166 Palms

- a - literary - anthology -

2017

ISBN-10: 1541275004
ISBN-13: 978-1541275003

CONTENTS

FORWARD

Beloved and memorable, the one hundred and sixty-six Canary Island Date Palms that welcome students and visitors to Stanford University are perhaps the most iconic of the four hundred species and over twenty-thousand individual trees growing on campus. Imagine for a moment that these *Phoenix canariensis* symbolize the bringing together of diverse and gifted learners united in the pursuit of inspiration and discovery. Could it be this indelible spirit then influenced the development of Stanford University's unique novel writing program where prestigious Stegner Fellows carefully select and mentor aspiring writers from all over the world? Embrace the possibility and discover an anthology inspired by these very ideals, an anthology celebrating the unique voices of extraordinary writers, an anthology appropriately titled, *166 Palms.*

—James Burnham ('14), Editor

CRIB BITING

by Stacey Swann

Sophie normally drove straight past Granger. The horse's pasture was a quarter mile from the house, and she'd speed by, the car throwing gravel up from the dirt road, not seeing him even as she looked right at him. But today she rounded the corner and caught Granger in the act. She put the Suburban in park, rolled down her window, and watched. There was something familiar in the rhythm of his actions, something she couldn't place. The horse pulled back his suede lips, exposing teeth and pale gums, stretched his jaw open, and placed his upper teeth on the top of the fence post. His neck arched, muscles contracting as he inhaled chunks of air and then exhaled in long grunts. Sophie's brain dragged up the connection. Granger reminded her of an Olympic deadlifter when he reached the weight he could not budge, the strength of his arms not able to defeat the inertia of all those pounds. Just replace the horse with a squatting Bulgarian, the teeth with taped and powdered hands. The grunting noise was identical.

"Try a smaller post," she called to him. The horse stopped, his teeth still lodged in the wood, and eyed her. Then he began again.

Sophie's husband would have blamed the pills for her delay in recognizing the link between horse and athlete. They had seen a Swedish author on *Charlie Rose* talk about how antidepressants curbed his ability to make analogies. Sophie thought it bullshit. It wasn't the Effexor, she just hadn't watched Olympic weightlifting for thirty years. *She* was not the one who mislabeled cause and effect.

"Where you off to?" Ed appeared—from which direction, she didn't know—and stood by the car window.

"Groceries. Doctor's appointment." For the past week, Ed had missed the same spot shaving, and now there was a small fur scab under his jaw. It bothered her, but since he had enough jutting chin for two men, it was hard for him to see around it.

"Already, again?" he said. His forearm lay across the car's open window, but he looked at Granger instead of her.

"Already again," she repeated, making her tone upbeat for no reason. "Shall I bring the psychiatrist home? Ask if he'll make a house call for a horse with addiction problems?"

"Pills for everybody," said Ed, mirroring her tone. Granger grunted, a strangled choking sound. In truth, Sophie was losing confidence in her doctor, though she'd never admit that to Ed, who had no confidence in the man from the start. He had just switched her to a third type of antidepressant, but none of them did more than lift her to the almost-surface of her sadness, where everything was muffled. To feel little was better, she knew, than to feel awful. But she couldn't call it a cure—only a variation on the theme.

"He's thinner. Is the list exhausted yet?" she asked.

Home remedies for a neurotic horse: place a mirror nearby to distract him (or if worried about breaking glass, try a large horse poster), surround him with chickens or goats, coat the post with a spray made from habanero peppers. Ed had moved on to mail order cures—a cribbing collar, leather connected by a fat metal hinge which pinched Granger's throat.

"The list is now officially exhausted," Ed said. The horse was flexing his neck as if unconstrained.

"Maybe he's just a masochist."

They had gotten Granger back from his trainer, his racing career never breaking past Manor Downs and the Gillespie County Fairgrounds. His pedigree was enough to get an occasional stud fee, so Ed wouldn't geld him. Instead, he had leased this parcel of adjacent land and fenced it off. The closest Granger could get to their mares was fifty yards. After a few months, with nothing to do but graze and find new ways to trigger endorphins, he began this crib biting, this windsucking. Sophie had attempted research—there were websites devoted to the discussion of sad horses. Cribbing and perimeter pacing and weaving, where a horse would sway its head back and forth like an autistic child rocking himself. Sophie started to feel slightly sick reading about it. Since Ed avoided the internet, their son, still at Texas A&M, did the research and mailed Ed the list.

"Granger's not a masochist," Ed told her. "He's just developed a harmful crutch."

Sophie was going to bring up Ed's cigar habit but sighed instead. "It's barely past noon. Why aren't you at school?"

"The Assistant Principal is covering my auto mechanics class. June got out again yesterday, and I needed to check the fences."

"Did you find the hole?"

"Isn't one."

"She's practicing for steeplechase?" Sophie turned up her radio.

"There isn't a hole."

"You're too old to not know how to shave," she said. Ed fell into his instinctual response when confronted by confusing information—he took a step back. Sophie rolled up the window and put the car into gear.

There was a grocery store in town, fifteen minutes from their home. But it didn't sell capers or truffle oil, and its fruit was often halfway-past ripe. Sophie drove the forty minutes to a Whole Foods in Houston. Plus, it was close to her doctor's. Their town was too small to boast a psychiatrist. When she had reached her lowest, unwilling to let Ed pull her from the floor of their walk-in pantry, unable to stop crying or explain even why she was crying, her husband had forced her to their GP in town. The old doctor had held the sample pack of Prozac out to her, gingerly gripping it, as if it was as dangerous as the mercury once used to treat syphilis. Or, as if he feared its mysterious power. Thus far, Sophie had found them less than powerful.

By the time Sophie came home, it was almost dusk. The winter clouds were so thick, the light didn't dim so much as evaporate. This was her excuse for almost running over Ed, who stood in the middle of the road with his hand out like a traffic cop. She rolled down the window and shouted, "What?"

"Quiet," he said. He turned his back to her but stayed in the road. Sophie joined him and they faced June who stood on the other side of the cattle guard, a grid of parallel pipes over a shallow ditch. She put one hoof down with a metallic clank. The mare took another step, placing her hoof with deliberate care—the front of it on one pipe and the back on another. Ed flinched with each step. "She's going to break her goddamn leg."

"Stop her."

"Wouldn't it be safer to let her cross?" he said.

June took two more careful steps and then jumped the last section, landing safely a few feet in front of them. She blew a stream of air from her nose and tried to canter past, but she didn't dodge around Ed quickly enough. He caught her halter and pulled her back in the other direction.

"Well," said Sophie, breaking up a clump of mud in June's mane. "Ten acres and a barn, and she still isn't satisfied." Ed had grown up on this land, in this same house. In those years before Sophie knew them, Ed's father had slowly rid the place of all its livestock—first the horses, then the pigs, then the chickens. Not worth the trouble, he repeated each time. She could see the dead man's point.

Sophie made rosemary crepes with Gruyère. She once enjoyed the complicated yet orderly steps of cooking, the art of time management. Now even new dishes seemed rote. After dinner, she settled at the computer while Ed settled at the TV. She had struck up an internet friendship with a Canadian from the sad horse site. He had cured his own horse of her weaving and he lived outside of Kingston, a place Sophie had visited as a child. That shared piece of geography was enough to form a link, and they had written about the Thousand Islands, how perfect it would be to own a vacation home on one of those tiny chunks of land sprinkled down the Saint Lawrence River. The winter was really setting in, and he had sent her pictures of the ice crusting across the river. Having lived for years by the Brazos, which never stopped moving, Sophie was unsettled by the visual of a river icing, shrinking from the sides. She knew she was more unsettled than she should be. She deleted the email and blocked his address.

Ed leaned in the doorway. "Could you try another search?" he asked.

"Too overwhelming. Too much to sift through."

"Maybe Dustin missed something."

"Doubt it," she said. But Ed didn't move away. "Where's the list he made?" she asked. Her husband pulled a worn piece of paper from his back pocket, folded into quarters. She smoothed it out on the desk as Ed looked over her shoulder. Big red exes covered all the options. Their son had not put antidepressants on the list, even though Sophie had seen it listed as a possible cure on the internet.

"Maybe there's some new thing. Something that's come up since Dustin searched."

Sophie went to Google and typed *cutting edge windsucking cures.* "Nope," she said.

"Soph." He used a tone of exasperation, one that used to please her. She loosened up the search terms. Then she turned on the CD player and started to sing loudly along with John Conlee. The tactic worked, driving Ed from his hovering and back into the living room—too easy to turn his reserve against him, make weapons of inconsequential things.

She focused her search on antidepressant use in horses but soon learned they weren't particularly effective. Perhaps that was why her son had left it off. More likely, though, Dustin knew his father's opinion, which meant they must have discussed her. She felt spiked by an irrational hurt.

The next morning, she woke at five and couldn't go back to sleep. She brought her face within an inch of Ed's shoulder and, in the dimness, she tried to see his skin as she used to see it. She tried to remember what she once thought his skin contained.

On Saturday, Sophie walked to the pasture and found Ed talking to their neighbor Gary. She and June stood at the edge of the cattle guard, both of them staring at a chain affixed to the fence post on one side and clipped to a hook on the other. June stretched out her nose and tapped the chain, making it sway.

"So, what?" she said to her husband. "We've got to stop, get out, undo the chain, drive across, get out, and put the chain back up? Doesn't that defeat the purpose of the cattle guard?"

"Pretty amazing June will do it, though. Yeah?" said Gary. He spoke louder than normal. Gary became squeamish around anyone's displeasure.

"Amazing," echoed Sophie. "Bizarre and amazing." She watched Granger eat grain from his bucket tied to the fence. "Maybe we can teach Granger to walk on water."

"Ed was telling me he hasn't been grazing as much because of the cribbing. He does seem thinner."

Sophie turned to June, rubbed her palm up and down the horse's forehead. She could tell neither of them enjoyed it much.

"What brings you down?" Ed asked her. She placed her hand on June's neck and stared at him.

"How you been, Sophie?" Gary tried. "How's the Chamber of Commerce?"

"An exercise in futility. But at least answering the phone isn't overwhelming." She forced a smile. "Want to stay for dinner? Fried catfish."

"Tempting," said Gary. "But Jo's in town for the weekend, and I'm supposed to take her the new Chinese place. You two should come with us." Gary turned from Sophie to Ed and back. Ed leaned down and uprooted a clump of Johnson grass. Sophie looked at June.

"I heard she wound up moving to Austin. That right?" said Sophie.

Gary nodded. "Applying to a PhD program there."

"Tell her I said hello." Sophie gave a last look at the chain, then her husband, before heading back to the house.

Though Ed never complained about her cooking, she could tell he was pleased to find something familiar on his plate. He ate two servings of fish and smeared pats of butter on the hush puppies. Sophie even served the canned creamed corn he liked. She left most of her own uneaten.

For years, she had gotten a secret pleasure from causing Ed's weight to balloon and deflate by fluctuating the calorie content of their meals. A week of feast followed by a week of famine without him even noticing the difference. She liked the power she felt when Ed looked at his straining shirt buttons in confusion. Now she saw she could have achieved the same goal with little effort by weaving in his childhood favorites instead. She felt robbed and ridiculous. Then restless.

"I've got to run an errand."

"Now? Everything's closed."

"Truck stop's still open. I won't be long."

"What do you need from the truck stop?"

"Lottery tickets? Porn? Cigarettes?"

Ed pushed back from the table, but she got up and turned away, no answer for his quizzical face. She drove, made it a quarter mile past their property before she had to pull over, all her energy gone. She left her car for the side of the road, crouching down in the ditch, in the dark. She slid her hands into the tangled brown of the dead grass. After thirty seconds, she felt better enough to feel foolish, so she stood and cut through a small stretch of woods to the fence line of Granger's pasture. The horse was still, thirty yards away, head turned in her direction. After a few silent minutes, she heard Ed's boots crossing the cattle guard. The gate to the pasture rattled open, and he came toward the horse, not noticing her standing on the other side of the fence. He talked to Granger, low smooth words she could not make out, and then he gripped the horse's head, his fists curling around the bases of the long soft ears. The horse made a noise like a sigh, and Ed rested his forehead between Granger's wide-spaced eyes.

Sophie wondered who was getting comfort from the exchange. She decided she didn't care.

Sophie again woke up near five. She dressed and went outside, walking down to the bank of the river, listening to cows lowing downstream. The sun wasn't even close to rising, but the pink-orange smudge of Houston lay to the east—the constellations blurring away at its edges. She hadn't looked at the river in the dark for years. She didn't feel anything but the wind. She knew feeling nothing wasn't right, wasn't normal either, but it no longer bothered her. The feeling made time speed up, made the passing of weeks feel like the passing of days.

She started down the road, thought she could get in a walk before the sun came up, but when she reached Granger's pasture, she saw him sitting in the middle of it like a dog: his forelegs bracing up his weight, his back legs splayed against the dirt. She watched him for a few minutes, not thinking of anything, and finally, she turned back for the house. She flipped on lights as she went in: porch light, kitchen light, hall light, bedroom light. Ed sat up, pulling the covers up and over his eyes.

"What?" A wet spot from his sleeping-drool brushed against his nose.

"Granger is sitting in the dirt. His rump is on the ground, but he's not lying down."

"Colic." Ed threw back the sheets.

"Colic?"

"From the cribbing, getting air in his intestines. Call the vet." He left the bed and was dressed and gone before Sophie found the number.

When she joined him in the pasture, at first she only saw her husband. Then she saw legs thrashing in the air, Granger's body blocked from view by a mesquite tree. The horse lifted himself off the ground, sweating despite the coldness of the morning. Ed slipped a halter and lead onto the horse and left his hand on Granger's head. He said, "It's okay. It's okay. Vet will be here soon."

Ed pulled back the horse's lips to check his gums—dry and red instead of smooth and pink. He pressed a fingertip into the flesh and for a long time the color did not return. Granger pawed at the ground and whipped his head around to stare at his own side. Ed sagged, miserable and helpless and small next to the horse.

"Vet's on the way," Sophie said. "Might be an hour."

The horse tried to drop back to the ground to roll, but Ed pulled hard on the lead and walked him in a circle. "Looks bad," he said. She knew he was trying to catch her eye, but she kept staring at a live oak at the far end of the field, its leaves shaking in the wind while all the other trees had bare branches. Sophie wondered what was missing in her brain, why she could not recognize it as pretty. Ed dropped the lead, and Granger lowered himself to the ground.

"If you don't need me, I'm going back to the house," she said. She turned, but before she could walk away, she felt Ed's arms circle her waist. He held her against him, his chin tucking around the side of her neck. As he hugged her, both of them utterly still, something inside buckled and gave.

SHOOTING STARS

by Kenton Yee

Following another solar flare, new swarms of space mites, like cirrocumulus clouds, pock the yellow-orange sky over the San Gabriel Mountains. They are driving me nuts.

I follow my sister Dahlia into the back seat of the patrol car. A cop's driving us to the station. Nobody Mirandized us, but he confiscated my .357 Glock. The cop steers with his left hand and squeezes a mic like a gun with his right. "Paul one-one-four en route." A 9-millimeter Beretta shimmers under his right armpit, a star ready to shoot. He clips the mic back on its dashboard holster. Dispatch belches back numbers.

Arms crossed, Dahlia is silent and shaking in a mohair sweater, alert as a wet cat. I lay an arm around her shoulders. My sister doesn't pull away. It feels awkward. We've never been touchy. I have no kids and can't know how Dahlia feels. Fact is, I've been celibate since high school. You know how it is for code monkeys. I drank a lot of Mountain Dew. Two gazillion lines of code later, seven years are gone. My mouth is dry as sand in the sun. I sure could use a Dew now.

Our driver slaps his cheek. "Gotcha!"

I watch.

His silhouette rolls something too small to see between the thumb and index finger before flicking it toward the empty passenger's seat. "Damn space mites," he says. "Annoying, aren't they?"

"Yup." I know better than to chat up a cop, especially when I may become the prime suspect in a missing boy case. Anything I say might incriminate me, right? I know because Dad was a homicide detective. He taught me the police code. Paul one-one-four is our cop's ID. Ten-twenty-five is child abuse. Ten-fifty-four is a corpse. Dad wore a three fifty seven Glock. During fights, he aimed it at Mom, whispered "boom," and laughed uproariously. When I was in high school, Mom went missing. She made us breakfast that morning. I came home from school to find the egg-stained dishes unwashed in the sink and no Mom. Reporters camped out in front of our house and pointed accusing microphones in Dad's face. Two weeks later, Dad pointed the Glock to his ear and pulled the trigger. I found his ten-fifty-four after school. His brain splattered all over my Milky Way bedspread and 12.5 inch telescope. I've coped, more or less.

"My wife sucked one down her throat when jogging," the cop says. "Doc tells her that the space mites are harmless. They'd better be. We're surrounded with'em."

I use my noncommittal voice. "They ride down on solar flares like shooting stars."

Dahlia peers at me with an admonishing stare, as if we are out of line to chitchat about mites when her son Jimmy, my only nephew, is missing. What Dahlia doesn't know is that a space mite might be responsible. One buzzed into my right earhole last month at the shooting range while I was adjusting my earmuff. After that, I couldn't aim straight. I went home and sat in my backyard jabbing my earhole until sundown. The mite wouldn't leave. Since then, I've poked and jabbed with fingers, pens, and coat hangers. I need a cotton tip, but I don't want to pay for a whole box.

Dahlia doesn't know any of this. To her, I'm just the lackadaisical orphan brother she raised after Dad died. She phoned last night asking me to spend an afternoon with little Jimmy at the mall. "He needs a father figure," she said.

Do I trust my mite near Jimmy? I feigned a prior commitment.

"You pretend to buy him a toy for Christmas," she said. "I'll pay you back and buy lunch."

So my sister didn't believe I'd get my nephew a present on my own accord? I was offended, but I couldn't turn down free food. Maybe snag a cotton tip at the makeup counter. After we split a lemon herb chicken at the food court, Dahlia dashed off to buy discounted intimates. "Keep your eye on Jimmy," she said.

The boy eyed me with suspicion. Did Jimmy want froyo? Nope. Did Jimmy want to pee pee? Nah.

I frowned.

He slurped.

My earhole tickled. I winked. "Want a present, Jimbo? It's out of this world."

He shrugged.

I walked behind him and pressed my right ear over his left, hard. He wiggled and pulled away. But the mite was too fast. It had buzzed from my earhole into his.

Yup.

I was so relieved to be rid of the thing, I stood with my eyes shut, jabbing and stirring, stirring and jabbing my evacuated earhole.

"Where's Jimmy?"

I opened my eyes to see Dahlia carrying a fluffy shopping bag. "He's right here—" I said without looking.

"Where?!"

Uh oh.

Dahlia's pupils shrank. Jimmy had gone missing. She dropped her fluffy bag and clawed the air futilely, legs rooted like redwoods in a thunderstorm. What lungs! Her shriek, as true as Mom's whenever Dad glocked her, thrummed my eardrums. All the force of our parents' tragedy must have whooshed through Dahlia's lungs. By comparison, the next three hours were quiet as cotton. She jabbed the chests of mall cops, shoved aside strangers with kids resembling Jimmy, and stirred every large shopping bag with a bare forearm.

I hid tears.

Now, we are listing left and right on the imitation leather seats like tethered buoys. "I don't understand," she mumbles for the tenth time. "How could a boy vanish inside Millennia Mall?"

"Security is reviewing the videos," I say, not without apprehension. Dahlia might never speak to me again if they show them to her.

"What were you doing when Jimmy ran off?" Dahlia says.

"Auhmm–" I say. "I think I was—"

Blaaaaaaaaaaack! The radio in the patrol car snaps us to attention. "Ida-one-two reports a ten fifty-four, Caucasian, purple windbreaker, green pants, red Keds, in Millennia Mall. Two-one-four-eight, over."

Ten fifty-four? My heart sinks.

Dahlia's body tenses. She leans forward. "Green pants, red Keds! That's Jimmy!"

The copper squeezes the mic. "Ten four. I have the mother and uncle with me. Paul one-one-four." He sticks the mic back in its holster and clicks off the static.

Dad never taught Dahlia the police code. She doesn't know that a ten fifty-four is bad news. The worst.

Her eyes narrow. She frowns. "What's a ten fifty-four?"

"They'll explain everything at the station, ma'am," the cop says, staring straight ahead.

"Omigod! Omigod!" Dahlia's voice is so loud it hurts my eardrums. "Is Jimmy okay?"

The red sky is muddy; the mite clouds, clumpy. My throat is thunder. My voice, gone.

There is only one thing to do.

I lift my arm off Dahlia, straighten the index finger, and poke it into my earhole. Like Dad did. I cock my thumb and pull the trigger. "Boom," I whisper, just loud enough to get Dahlia's attention.

I see stars. My head snaps sideways in slow mo. My hand recoils in the opposite direction.

For the first time since finding Dad, I love my sister, I do.

The cop unleashes the windshield wipers.

The raindrops keep coming.

BOUNDARIES

by Luanne Castle

With the peak of its A-frame pointing skyward toward our heavenly goal, the First Methodist Church marked the entrance to the neighborhood. Oaks and pine trees shed their acorns and needles on the churchyard. Squirrels and birds made their homes outside the stained glass window. Church leaders had installed one swing set and one seesaw next to the big parking lot and called them a playground. Crabapple trees, which bordered the lot, tempted bored children with their hard, bitter fruit.

My parents and brother and I lived a lazy walk down the street from the church. As I approached my teen years, I refused to walk side by side with them after services, but plowed ahead, head bent and watching my Kelly green patent leather pumps rotate beneath me. "Where you going so fast, Lu?" Dad called out.

Mom had let me wear nylons, and my feet slid around in the low-heeled pumps. My little brother ran past me, his short brown hair ruffling in the breeze. "Slowpoke!" he called. I felt as if I were rising up like a crocus out of the earth, bursting with expectation.

The summer I turned thirteen, at the boundary of our backyard, my parents planted a garden of tomatoes, string beans, and zucchini. Next door, the old man's garden soil was darker and richer. His tasseled corn could be eaten crisp off the cob. Adjacent to our garden was my tether ball court and on the other side of the concrete slab, the playhouse my father had built me smiled its crescent moon grin. Dad's joke was that crescent moons used to mark outhouses when he was a kid.

Along the back boundary of the houses on the other side of my street was a forest of Balsam firs and white pines known as "The Pines." At one end of the pines was the church and, at the other end, the minister lived in the parsonage with his wife, my piano teacher. Below my scales and arpeggios, I could hear the junior high boys playing softball outside. The timbre of the boys' voices called me to come play with them.

Under the trees, the earth was two inches thick with fallen needles. My friends and I hauled our sleeping bags out there for summer sleepovers, and sometimes Karen's brother and his friends visited. Warm nights increased the pungent fragrance of the pine needles, which blended with the spicy scent of the teen boys.

One night, Karen's thirteen-year-old stepbrother kissed me and lay down beside me on my sleeping bag.

He smelled like nothing I'd ever smelled, but I liked it. In the midst of a carpet of cricket chirps, an animal beeped.

"What's that?" I giggled.

"It might be a tree frog. And the rest are crickets."

"I had a pet cricket in fourth grade." He was so close to me that I could smell his breath. I'd known him for three years and had stayed overnight at their house plenty of times.

He lay on top of me, resting his length against mine. His mouth was a rock warm from the sun. A tiny bristle like sandy grit bit my upper lip. The other kids had paired off, as if we had partitioned into small separate countries.

When Karen's brother and I finished kissing, he got up and pulled me to my feet. Within moments, we all ran under the stars, armed with toilet paper to decorate shrubs and cars.

The next day the boys played ball in the street and ignored my friends and me as we sat on the curb, talking and laughing and pretending the boys weren't within yelling distance.

This tacit agreement went on for weeks. Every day, our 1st and 2nd grade brothers, testing how far they could push us, rode by on their Schwinn Stingrays and Huffy bicycles, tossing insults at us. Skanks. Turds. What could they know?

After dinner one night, we girls decided to bring our sleeping bags to the playhouse. We played Candy Land with flashlights, but the cramped space was hot and we kept sticking our hands in spider webs, so we moved our sleeping bags out behind the playhouse. As we lay on our backs and looked up, we saw the moon pregnant with meaning above us.

When the boys arrived, they had a new friend with them. He could have been the good-looking blond star of a 1950s juvenile delinquent movie. One of my other friends had decided she liked Karen's brother, so when the others paired off, Blondie and I were left facing each other. We all knew why the boys were here and why we had expected them to come.

“Hey.” His top lip curled back, revealing large teeth.

He smelled like peaches warming in a sunny window. “Hey.” My voice sounded tinny.

He was our age but looked older. The others moved further into the field, so that they became dark shapes in the near distance. He pulled me to him with one arm. I never thought of resisting.

Blondie's kiss started out like those of Karen's brother, but within moments he thrust a fat, wet, wiggling thing in my mouth. It took me a moment to realize it was his tongue. He pressed me down to the ground and lay on top of me. His tongue was a powerful saltwater animal. His mouth was all over my face. Weed stalks and small stones jutted into my back through the thin sleeping bag.

He redirected his efforts to the double stitched inseam of my jeans, pushing and rubbing into the soft unknown place between my legs. His hands were so rough, so forceful, that I felt pain as he continued to push.

Everywhere his body touched me was an intrusion, as if he invaded, not just my body, but also my mind. As he pushed me, I felt the force of his strength, his solidity and weight. My breath came shallow and quick, and a sense that I was suffocating agitated my stomach. Still, I was silent, struggling not to disconnect my mind from my body.

"Stop." My cry was barely audible, but I pushed back at him, eventually shoving him off me. Without speaking or looking at me, he grabbed a handful of tall weeds, yanked, and then broke them into pieces, pretending that nothing had happened.

Within minutes, the boys decided it was time to go. My friends waved at the boys, and the boys waved back. I didn't raise my hand. I just stared after them. I had entered a world separate from my girlfriends, as if from that night on, nothing was a certainty.

School started a few days later, and Blondie turned up in my English class. I refused to look at him. He sat in the back row and joked loudly with another boy. A couple of weeks into the semester, our teacher went to the office while we worked on an assignment. We were reading, searching for favorite poems for the poetry scrapbooks she had assigned. I had fallen headfirst into an Edna St. Vincent Millay poem when, suddenly, I felt a steel grip on my crotch. Looking down, I saw a hand shoved in between my legs. The hand belonged to an arm with blond hairs. The arm belonged to Blondie.

"Get away!" I threw his arm away from me. The classroom around me grew tight and mirrored, with bodiless faces replicated ad nauseam, all staring at me. I refused to look at him as he sauntered back to his seat, but I could feel the smirk at my back.

As I walked home from school with my friends, I tuned them out as they hashed over the day about who was kicked out of study hall for smoke bombs in the boys' bathroom.

Karen asked me why I was so quiet. I must have been in shock; my chattiness and giggling had abandoned me. I listened to the girls around me, feeling as though I were in the empty middle of the ring of life. In that emptiness, I found the blistering wheel of humiliation.

I heard a male voice behind us. "You can run, but you can't hide." Looking back, I saw Blondie shadowing us, sauntering, his books carried at his hip. The toxic gas of dread filled my body as it were a balloon.

My friends giggled. "Maybe he likes you." Karen poked my waist. I ignored her. Nobody really knew him or where he had come from. We kept walking, ignoring Blondie, until I saw him mosey up the steep driveway and into a ranch house. It didn't take us long to get to our street.

For weeks afterward, I surrounded myself with girlfriends, making sure I was never alone. In class, I kept a heavy textbook open on my lap. Nevertheless, Blondie managed two more times to bolt across the aisle and up several seats to grab me. Each time I slapped him away. He sneered and, the second time, he winked. While I burned with humiliation, the other students now kept their noses in their books. Did they really not see what was happening? Or were they colluding with him?

The fourth time, venom burst in my stomach. I was blind to the exterior world and reacted with the poison rising within me. I slapped his face. My hand hurt. Even his jawbone was hard, sharp, a danger to me. But he pulled back, surprised. Some students had looked up at the crack of my hand on his gritty oil-paper cheek.

That afternoon, we girls kept to our regular route, walking down the main street where the cars buzzed by. With the shame so thick inside me, I couldn't confide in my friends, but they were now used to my silence. They let me lag a step behind. The whoosh and blast of wind as each car passed us made me sway. Unsteady, I planted my feet heavier and heavier on the sidewalk with each step. Some leaves still hung from the oak branches above, as I crunched through the fallen dead leaves. How had I missed the brilliant reds and yellows of the trees the past few weeks?

As my friends turned toward the church and waited for a lull in the traffic, I caught sight of a squirrel lying under a large oak on someone's front lawn. I ran toward the animal, without a word to the girls. Kneeling on the grass, I took in the squirrel's graceful muzzle and nose, noted the dull black of its eyes.

A moment later, I noticed that the gut had burst—whether from a predator or not, I didn't know, but the legs and luxurious tail appeared as if the animal were alive. The squirrel's innards were open to view, like the plastic models of human anatomy in our science classroom. Rather than an illuminating glimpse, the flesh moved as if the squirrel were alive deep down inside. A half-beat later, I realized a mass of larvae writhed, working diligently on the dead tissue. I'd never seen death or what comes after. Now I witnessed the dead squirrel changing, in process of becoming.

I knew from science class that the maggots, though revolting, were necessary to the cycle of life. I shivered in recognition, as if I were witnessing something I had sensed was going on inside of me.

"Eew, disgusting." Karen had followed and stood over me, her shadow falling to the right of the carcass. She tugged on my shoulder. "Come on."

Reluctantly, I rose, willing myself to look once more at the squirrel's face, rather than the maggot infestation. Karen and I crossed the main street that separated our neighborhood from the city, joining the others who waited for us on the sidewalk. When a girl asked why we ran to the tree, Karen spoke without emotion. "Dead squirrel." Neither of us mentioned the maggots. We trudged past the church, marking our path home--through the parking lot, around the pines that never lost their color, and down the street toward our houses.

FAMILY BUSINESS

by Victoria Grant

You and Felicia had only just knelt down at the lower bunk bed, reciting in matching cadence "Now I lay me down to sleep—" when Mama barged through the door, shouting, "What the *hell* you think you're doing? You little bitches had all week to memorize that goddamn Lord's Prayer. Lemme hear it." She pounded a ham-like fist on the top bunk bed. "Now, dammit, now!"

Felicia's shudder matched your own: chilled, spiky fingers tripping down your spine. Your flesh pimpled up, a perverse reaction to Mama's hot flares of temper, and tears welled up, ready to spill over. Mama snarled, "Want me to give you a good reason to cry?" You struggled to hold back, choking down the sobs, lips pressed together as if super-glued through eternal years of practice. You were six years old.

While your five-year-old sister brandished a frozen stare, you clasped your prayerful hands tighter. Mama's angry face wore piggly eyes, a long, wart-ladened nose, and thin bloodless lips pinched to express foul words meant to scorch your heart.

Or was that Snow White's stepmother? Would that kind woodcutter or seven helpful little people come save you in the nick of time? Would anyone's eardrum spasm from your shrieks of pain and terror this time? Where's *your* prince? Where's Daddy? Not here. Maybe at work; with friends. Somewhere. He'll be back. Eventually.

There used to be a time when Daddy seemed happy to be with you. He teased you in a way that didn't hurt your feelings. *Where's Daddy's big girl? Tell me about your day. Did that little boy try to kiss my princess again? You tell him you're Daddy's girl, and he has to ask my permission.* Then he tickled Felicia, sputtered little kisses around her neck, because he loved her, too. At dinner, everyone talked with everyone, and Daddy smiled at Mama, bragged about her cooking, boasted all of you were the best family a man could have. Afterwards, he was never too tired to play with you, help tuck you into bed, and watch over like a guardian angel while you said your prayer. The one Mama and Daddy taught you from your first babbling words, mimicking each syllable: "Now I lay me down to sleep...."

Something changed over time. Mama and Daddy never told you what happened. You began to observe them in a secret way, closer, studying them while playing with Felicia or your dolls. You had to see for yourself the changes that made your lives sadder. Like Daddy missing dinners. After a while, you didn't see him until bedtime, and sometimes not even then. Who to talk to about these new, strange ways of theirs? Felicia was too young to understand, except in a way, you know she did. She seldom cried or spoke anymore.

How could Mama and Daddy ignore their rising voices when you were supposed to be asleep? What were those words about: Other woman? Outside child? You never spoke with Felicia about their heart-bursting anger, but you heard her whimpering on the bottom bunk. Big girls didn't whimper – but, still, you didn't sleep too well.

Daddy still lived at home, under the same roof, but only attached to you by the slimmest of familial threads. Sometimes, he came home after your bedtime, and, like the magician at your friend's birthday party, disappeared, gone before you awoke in the morning. You began to look forward to weekends when he slept later, and you regaled him with stories about your day while he sipped his coffee. Listening to the stay-in-place comforting sounds of his washing and shaving, you shouted through the closed bathroom door that you still punched the little boy who tried to kiss Daddy's princess. Right after breakfast, you bawled while tugging his pant legs, pleading with him not to leave. He wouldn't promise when – or if – he'd return. Mama would try to pull you off. You clung on like those little burrs in the woods attached to your summer clothes. Then, finally, frustrated, Mama slapped your hands away.

Now, you dared a darting glance upwards at a frumpy Mama wearing a drab housedress. She was backlit by the hallway ceiling light, her corpulent frame hovering. The frothing earthy aroma of her sweating body forced you to breathe only through your mouth. When you were a real family, Mama glided through the house like an Ebony magazine model, trailing behind scented wafts of Chanel No. 5. She once bestowed upon you her empty perfume bottle, which you tucked in the back of your sock drawer. Overtime, the scent weakened, faded away along with memories of Mama's love.

At times, she really did seem like everyone else's Mama: she cleaned, fed and clothed you. She just didn't always act like everyone else's Mama. Your friends' mommies hugged them, kissed them, called them sweet names. Your Mama snatched you, smacked you, called you other names. Stupid. Ugly. Dirty. Clumsy. Lazy. Bitch.

Your friends never knew the way she was with you and Felicia. Mama warned you with a doomsday glare. You read in those eyes, "Better not tell." She said, "You don't put family business in the street."

Last week, the Sunday school teacher gave you and Felicia a half sheet of paper with the Lord's Prayer typed on it. Mama said, "Go to your room and memorize that shit." After a dozen readings, you and Felicia still had trouble with the strange words that tangled your tongues. It didn't sound right; not how you normally talked. *Now I Lay Me* was so easy, so smooth. Your prayerful reward, sweet dreams. Also, praying tasted like thin, crisp, wafer cones of soft ice cream custard. Chocolate.

Way back in vaporous time, Mama with a patient smile taught you to memorize. She broke down every few words to repeat after her.

"Now I lay me down to sleep. . ."

Now I lay me down to sleep. . .

"I pray the Lord my soul to keep…"

I pray the Lord. . .

Completing the recitation, you God-blessed everyone you could think of, ending with Mama, Daddy, and Felicia.

"Amen."

Ahhhmen.

You once asked, "Mama, why do I have to say this every night?" She said, "Because Daddy and I want you protected when we're asleep, too."

"That means I'll be safe?"

"Yes, that's right. Just like always."

Back then, Daddy stood in your bedroom doorway listening to you and Felicia chatting soft as spring rain. Pitter-patter chit-chat, he called it. His smile snuggled you in a love-cocoon soft as spun wool.

That was before the beginning of the loud talking that came before their angry shouting that came before their hurt-crying-whining that came before their ear-splitting quiet.

Everyone in your six to eight-year-old Sunday school group had to memorize the grownup Lord's Prayer by Palm Sunday. The class would recite it as a group. By rights, at five years old, Felicia didn't have to learn it until next year, but Mama said, "I'll be damned if I'm going through this shit twice. You two are trying enough on my nerves. Once is enough." You and Felicia decided to fake it Palm Sunday by moving your mouths, mumbling gibberish, unheard among the gathering. But, for the present, at this moment kneeling beside the bed, failure to obey meant certain punishment.

Together you chanted: "Our Father which . . . ." You stopped. Flashing through your mind, you recalled how you made fun of the next word, changing "art" to "fart." What did "which art in heaven" mean anyway? Helpless, you turned desperate eyes toward each other. Vision of the words on that half-page shimmered and blurred in your mind: meaningless words scattered on a piece of paper.

"Don't tell me you don't know…. Unh, unh, I don't *even* want to…. Don't give me this crap now. You stupid little fucks better not be shitting me now."

Mama stormed out the room, and you and Felicia exchanged a fearful glance. If you were lucky, she'd just yell, threaten, and curse at you.

As you feared, you weren't lucky. Mama returned with the thick leather belt, gripping the buckle end tightly. Wide as Daddy's fist, strong and supple from frequent use, it looked a lot like a barber's razor strop, except with a vertical string of small holes down the middle of one end. The belt inhabited the linen closet between two piles of bath towels, third shelf from the top, an easy reach for Mama. Heaven help you if it somehow got mislaid – Mama's angry hands found nearby objects to throw instead – so you no longer hid it to save yourselves from its biting kisses. The kids in 2C gave their father's belt a name. Their screams perforated the wall – "Oh no, Mr. Persuader, please no, Mr. Persuader. No more, Mr. Persuader." – and you sort of giggled, uncertain if their performance was tragic or funny. Mama's belt had no name; that would be like giving it personality, making friends with it, pleading with it to stop hurting you. How useless.

The belt hung as long as your arm from Mama's hand. Holding it from the buckle end meant a lesser pain. And at least it wasn't her alternate favorite, the old steam iron cord with its center of thin metal wiring. You silently prayed, *Maybe she won't use it. Maybe she's too tired. Maybe I'll remember the words; I did read them a few times.*

"Now say it, damn you. Our Father which art in heaven . . . ."

"Our Father which art in heaven . . . ."

Silence. Your unspoken prayer had gone unanswered. The sudden hush was a knife that sliced away your salvation.

Mama's first backswing of the strap cut you on your left arm. Then she lifted the belt and flashed down again, cutting into Felicia's right. The sound it made on your bodies was like that of a cleaver hacking off fish heads on a butcher block. An inferno streamed down the strike lines, and you cried out like a child-sized demon. Rubbing an injured arm with one hand and wiping at your eyes with the other, you remained kneeling. So did Felicia. The both of you cringed, each like a crippled praying mantis, but you didn't dare budge from the standard position of prayer

"Now say it again. Our Father which art in heaven, hallowed be thy name."

"Our Father which art in heaven . . . hollow be the name . . . ."

Your brain stuttered to a halt. Felicia's eyes reflected your dread – you could not remember the next words.

There was the deliberate movement of Mama's raising arm. Your body stiffened like a crudely carved marionette, mind frozen into memory gridlock. You could not direct your thoughts to the correct words for anticipating the next swing. And that swing came, and came again. Through the thin layer of your pajamas, you suffered the strap's striping fire on your back, your legs, your arms. Tormented by your belief the suffering would never end, the memory lesson seemed to last for hours.

Felicia was the first to "remember" the whole Lord's Prayer. Allowed to scramble into bed and pull the cover over her head, never begging mercy for you.

Your guilt wouldn't let you stop loving Mama, but you think that's when you started hating Felicia. You hated the thing being done to you. You had to hate someone. Feared turned to anger, anger turned to hate. Sunday school taught you to honor your mother and father; it said nothing about sisters. Felicia was small and helpless against the fears simmering within you, the anger, always on the tipping edge of unpredictable eruption – maybe like Mama.

Mama and Daddy still loved you. They had pledged to protect you. And so you honored your parents, and showed your loyalty. You never told strangers about family business.

THE JOY OF CLUTTER

by Wendy Nelson Tokunaga

There was nothing wrong with him. He sat across from her at the Queen of Hearts *kissaten* in Ebisu, stirring cream into his coffee. His online picture resembled how he looked in real life so there'd been no surprises. He displayed no noticeable tics, and his weight was in proportion to his height. At thirty-five he had a full head of thick hair. His lips were thin, but not overly so, and his complexion was clear and free of moles. His teeth were fairly straight and any slight crookedness or hint of an overbite fell into the acceptable range.

He worked as a manager in the customer service division of a computer hardware company and earned a decent salary. On the weekends he enjoyed bowling, taking hikes and seeing movies. His favorite food was katsu curry and he preferred beer over sake, though he had nothing against the latter.

He was born in Tokyo and his name was…Ah! What was his name? She tried hard to remember. Shunya? Shinji? Shinzo? But as he talked on, she still couldn't recall. It was all a blur, like peering through the weakest lens during an exam at the eye doctor. And now the recorded music playing in the café seemed to get louder, drowning out his voice. An annoying buzzing took over her ears, becoming increasingly amplified to the point that it sounded like drones were flying overhead, drones that would start dropping bombs at any moment. But he kept talking and talking as if nothing were out of the ordinary, and when she just couldn't take *all the noise* any longer she finally shouted over the din, "I'm sorry, but I just remembered that I have an appointment. I need to go." And she got up too quickly and in her clumsiness nearly knocked over her iced green tea latte, but at last made it to the outside intact. She caught her breath and walked quickly toward Ebisu station without looking back.

Shunya-Shinji-Shinzo had been the twenty-first match she'd met in the last three months. She wasn't sure if she could take anymore.

. . .

"Eri-chan," her sister Saya was saying. "Don't you think it's time that you cleared out all this crap?"

Crap? It was such a harsh word, but Saya was well known for her blunt talk.

"You should do what I've done. You've heard of NoriMaki, right?"

"The sushi?" Eri said.

Saya sighed loudly.

No, Eri hadn't been living under a rock. She'd certainly heard of Noritake Maki. The decluttering guru was so famous that she was known by her abbreviated nickname NoriMaki. Her two books, *The Flutter of Declutter* and *The Flutter of Declutter Volume 2*, had sold millions of copies. She'd even recently branched out from Japan, becoming the premier tidy-up goddess in the United States. NoriMaki was a constant presence on television and in women's magazines. Even the ladies at Eri's work couldn't stop raving about the NoriMaki method. "Why haven't you tried it yet?" they'd ask. "It's magical!"

"Those books changed my life," Saya was saying now. "Seriously. Ever since I put the NoriMaki method into practice, things started happening for me. I'm telling you, you must read her books."

Saya had always been the neat freak of the two sisters, but this sounded extreme even for her. Eri hadn't seen her sister for over a year. She'd moved to Kobe with her husband and two-year-old daughter, while Eri still lived in Tokyo where the two had grown up. It was true that Saya's life had changed. She'd gotten married, had a baby and taken up yoga. She was slimmer than ever and wore her hair in a new short style that suited her well. Six months ago she started her own business, making and selling crocheted coin purses on the "d creators" online marketplace. Even her husband seemed like some kind of miracle. Although he had a full-time job, he managed to pitch in with the housework and childcare. At that very moment he was taking their daughter to Kiddy Land so the two sisters could spend time catching up.

"Look at all those books," Saya said, pointing to one of Eri's bursting shelves. "I bet you haven't even gotten around to reading half of them. And you never will. It's time to throw them out."

"But then you're telling me to buy *more* books."

Saya frowned. "NoriMaki's books are the only ones you'll need." She moved to the kitchen and flung open a cupboard. "And these? Just how many Disneyland mugs does one person need?"

"They're souvenirs," Eri said. One of her hobbies was visiting Tokyo Disneyland; she'd been there hundreds of times over the years. She was born on April 15, 1983, the day Tokyo Disneyland had opened. It was obviously some kind of sign. And by now she'd assembled quite a nice collection of mugs with designs of everything from Cinderella's Castle to Mickey and Minnie Mouse dressed in wedding costumes.

Eri took two mugs—both displaying Donald Duck's grinning face—and poured hot tea from the kettle. The two sisters sat at the small kitchen table.

"And you're still at Happy Yen," Saya said of the chain store where Eri worked as a supervisor in the lingerie and women's nightwear department. "How long has it been now?"

"Six years in September."

"And still no someone special?"

Eri shook her head. This was a fact as well. While Saya had been busy making changes, Eri had remained stuck. And, no, there was no husband, let alone boyfriend, on the horizon. There'd been Ryoji, but he was better left unmentioned. And that relationship had ended years ago. Men were not exactly banging down her door, which seemed to be the new normal once you were in spitting distance of your mid-thirties. Lately Eri had been going on arranged marriage meetings set up through an online matchmaking service, but nothing had yet to work out. She felt no spark for any of these men. There was a joyless sameness about them.

"You need to shake things up, Eri-chan," Saya said. "And that's what the NoriMaki plan can do for you."

Could a decluttering plan cause such big positive life changes? Eri was skeptical. And, besides, her small apartment wasn't cluttered, at least not in her eyes. She could find things when she needed them with no problem. She liked the warm feeling of her place, the coziness of having her possessions close by. Saya had texted photos of her living room. It looked more like the reception area of a day spa or a MUJI store display — stark and white. Cold.

Yes, maybe Eri did have some junk lying around, but she was far from being a hoarder. She was nothing like the elderly woman on the news whose son found her dead body underneath a mammoth pile of Pocky Chocolate Stick boxes.

Eri resisted following fads, which was difficult in a fad-mad country like Japan. That was one reason why she'd been trying hard to ignore NoriMaki. But maybe resistance was futile. She needed to change her life, that was for sure. The more she thought about it, the bleaker her future looked. If the NoriMaki method had worked for so many, certainly it could work for her. And what did she have to lose? A few thousand yen for a book?

So after Saya returned to Kobe Eri went to Kinokuniya and bought a copy of *The Flutter of Declutter* and read it one Sunday afternoon.

The overlying advice seemed to be to take stock of all your possessions and determine which ones gave you a feeling of *tokimeku*—in other words, making you palpitate, throb, or flutter inside. Did the item make you feel joyful or simply meh? This was the determining factor in deciding whether or not to throw it out.

It took a while, but Eri managed to gather most of her possessions in one overflowing pile in the middle of the living room floor. And as she went through them, one by one, something strange happened. They all gave her a spark of joy. Not one did she put in the "meh" pile. She whiled away the afternoon swooning over her magazines promoting the 30th anniversary of Tokyo Disneyland, the Banana Yoshimoto and Haruki Murakami novels she'd yet to read, the painting of a rising phoenix she'd bought in Hong Kong on a Golden Week vacation. The pink-colored tool kit her father had given her when she moved into her apartment; every Disneyland mug and commemorative plate; the jar of buttons she'd saved since she was seven years old; the plastic fruit with smiling faces Ryoji had bought her in Daikanyama as an apology for calling her a cranky old lady; the kendama toy she and Saya had fought over when they were children; a box of new year's cards, some from her grandmother who died in 2010. The twenty volumes of the "Hello Wedding" manga series; the cookbook written by celebrity chef Jun Komatsu that she'd bought, not for the recipes but for the sexy photos of him whipping cream; the ticket stubs for her first Kinki Kids concert. She wouldn't consider throwing any of these items out. All of them had special meanings, all held importance to her; every stuffed toy, key chain, perfume bottle, pair of socks, cell phone case and notebook.

Each and every one had made her want to sing with joy.

. . .

"Eri-chan, are you awake?"

Well, now she was awake. It was her mother's voice. Eri was twelve years old at the time, and her Chip and Dale clock had said two-forty-five in the morning.

"What's wrong?" Eri asked.

Her eyes adjusted to the darkness, and now she could see her mother, wearing a red sweater over her nightgown. She sat on the edge of Eri's bed, her hands folded in her lap. Was she sleepwalking? There was something ethereal and ghostlike about her appearance.

Or maybe she'd been drinking. There were times when her mother imbibed far too much plum wine. And that was usually when the fights with her father would start.

But Eri's mother had never come into her bedroom to talk to her in the middle of the night.

"First I get so cold and then I get so hot," her mother said, flinging off her sweater so that it landed on the floor. Eri's mother had been complaining about menopausal symptoms even though she was only forty-one. The family was forced to shiver when she opened all the windows in the middle of January, complaining of hot flashes that made her feel like she was trapped inside an oven.

But why would her mother need to discuss her body temperature at almost three o'clock in the morning? It was much too weird.

After a pause her mother said, "I need to tell you something, Eri-chan."

This sounded serious. Had she already been to Saya's room? Maybe not. Saya was two years younger. Perhaps, being the eldest, her mother had selected Eri to confide in.

"What is it, Mom? You're scaring me."

"Your father isn't your real father."

Eri sat up. "What?"

"I said your father isn't your real father." She stood and started pacing. "I got pregnant by someone else. He abandoned me when I told him, and shortly afterwards I met your father. He felt sorry for me, and we got married."

It sounded like something out of a home drama, not the true story of how you came into the world. Eri had always felt loved by her dad and never considered for a moment that he might not be her biological father.

"So who, who is my real father?"

"It doesn't matter."

"What do you mean, it doesn't matter?

"It doesn't matter because he's dead."

Eri felt liked she'd been punched in the chest.

Her mother returned to the edge of the bed.

"Why are you telling me this now?" Eri asked. "Are you and Dad breaking up?"

"No. I just felt like the time was right to let you know."

"But I was born on April 15, 1983, right?"

"Yes. Why?"

"I just wanted to make sure."

What a weird dream, Eri thought when she woke up the next morning. Her mother coming into her room in the middle of the night to tell her that her real father was dead and that the dad she'd known her whole life wasn't her father at all. A sense of relief came over her. Of course it wasn't true.

She sat up and stretched, thinking about the report due for science class the next day about black holes in the universe. Primordial black holes were the smallest. Next were stellar black holes that were twenty times larger than the sun. And then there were the gargantuan black holes located in the centers of galaxies, supermassive black holes that were more than one million times bigger than the sun.

She got out of bed and almost tripped over something that was strewn across the floor.

Her mother's red sweater.

. . .

It had never occurred to Eri to rent a middle-aged man, but desperate times called for desperate measures. What she wanted to talk about wasn't anything she could tell her co-workers or Saya or her old college friends. She wanted to be able to speak freely, and especially to not be judged. Talking to a complete stranger who expected nothing from you was more than just appealing; it was a necessity.

The *Rent an Ossan* web page indicated that all the men available were between 45 and 55 years of age and to rent one cost 1,000 yen per hour. The site took great pains to state that it was in no way promoting a dating or hook-up business. Eri had seen a television segment about how the service had been growing in popularity, particularly with young women. She understood how useful it might be to talk to an ossan you didn't know. So she made an appointment to meet with a Hamada-san one Saturday afternoon in Ueno Park on a bench near the museum.

The website had displayed a photograph of him, and Eri experienced a feeling of déjà-vu when she arrived at the park and searched for him, but thank God this wasn't another ridiculous match meeting. She recognized Hamada-san immediately. Perched on his head was the same gray beret he'd worn in his picture. She waved to him and he smiled and stood, motioning for her to sit next to him.

"Kawamura-san?" he said. "I am Hamada."

"Yes, nice to meet you. Thank you for agreeing to see me."

"It's my pleasure. How can I help you today?"

Eri explained how she'd bought the NoriMaki book after her sister had called her out about her junk.

"I see," said Mr. Hamada. "But you know that clutter in itself isn't a bad thing. Great works of art and other kinds of genius often come from some rather messy places."

"I don't think I'm particularly messy. It was just my sister who said so. But she's always been critical, ever since she was a little girl."

"And you've just taken it all in, haven't you?"

"Yes, I guess I have." Eri paused, thinking of how shortly after her mother's middle-of-the-night visit, Saya started to get rid of her vast collection of Japanese dolls, which had left her room essentially empty and soulless. Eri had rescued some of them from the garbage bin and hid them in her closet. And now they resided in a closet at her apartment.

"My sister said that once she purged her junk, good things began to happen for her."

"I see," said Hamada-san.

"I've been stuck in a rut for years. Same boring job, and no boyfriend for a long time now. And I've gone on too many matchmaking dates that have gone nowhere. So I decided to try the NoriMaki method. I read her book and followed the advice to the letter."

"And what happened?"

Eri paused. "Well, the funny thing was, every one of my possessions sparked a feeling of joy in me."

"Isn't that a good thing?"

Eri's lower lip trembled, and she started to cry.

Hamada-san didn't act shocked or surprised at Eri's outburst. Women becoming overly emotional probably happened often in his line of work. He patted her arm in an avuncular way.

"I'm sorry," Eri said, taking out a handkerchief from her purse and wiping her eyes, trying to regain her composure.

"Please don't apologize," Hamada-san said gently. "Take your time."

She explained that she'd been on twenty-one dates through the matchmaking service. "They were all perfectly reasonable guys. But not one of those men sparked any joy in me. There was no chemistry. And I just started to wonder…" She paused, wiping away more tears. "If there's, if there's something wrong with *me.*"

"Wrong with you?"

"Maybe I care more about material possessions than I do actual people."

Hamada-san was silent for a while, as if chewing on what she'd said. Did he think this was true, Eri wondered. Why wasn't he saying anything? She was hoping for some comfort, but maybe she'd hit the nail on the head. There was only one conclusion: she was shallow.

Finally Hamada-san spoke. "Kawamura-san, you are being much too hard on yourself. I think you need to stop taking the blame. There's nothing wrong with you. You are a passionate woman who is passionate about her things, passionate about life, a woman who does not settle for less. It just takes time to find the right person. You are not shallow for following your heart."

"You think so?"

"I know so."

. . .

In the next few weeks Eri went on several more appointments to see Hamada-san, discussing anything she could think of; how to deal with the employees she supervised, how to get along better with her boss, how to deflect her sister's criticism. Hamada-san always listened well and gave her thoughtful advice and support. She didn't know what she'd do without him.

But one day when she arrived for her appointment she saw that Hamada-san wasn't there. In his place was a man much younger, closer to her own age. Was it just a coincidence that he was sitting on the same park bench that had become their meeting place?

He looked at her as if he were expecting her. And then he spoke.

"Kawamura-san?" the man said.

"Yes?"

"My father could not come today so he sent me in his stead. I am Hajime Hamada."

Hajime wore stylish black-framed glasses, a gray pullover sweater, jeans and blue Converse high tops. He explained that his father was at home, that he'd been to the clinic because of anemia and low blood pressure, and his doctor had instructed him to rest for a week or so.

Eri insisted on visiting Hamada-san to wish him well. She and Hajime took a short train ride to Kanda to the house where Hajiime lived with his father, but not before Eri stopped at a kiosk in the train station to buy a package of fresh cream puffs to bring to him. Mrs. Hamada had died three years before and it was just the two of them, Hajime had explained. He said that he was an editor for a Japan travel magazine and sometimes worked from home. He told Eri how much his father loved his job as a rental ossan, and Eri said that she was grateful for his help and keen insights.

"You have a visitor," Hajime called out when they arrived at the gray house with a blue roof that had a sign that said "Hamada," and was a five-minute walk from the station.

Eri removed her shoes and stepped up to the entry way and into the living room where she saw Hamada-san sitting on the floor at a *kotatsu* table, a tan Chihuahua resting by his side. The dog was calm and only glanced at Eri and Hajime, preferring to stick close to Hamada-san's side.

"Ah! Kawamura-san," Hamada-san said, starting to rise.

"No, please, don't get up," said Eri. "I was so sorry to hear that you've been ill. Here's a little something." She handed him the box of cream puffs.

"I'll make tea," Hajime said and disappeared into the kitchen.

"Oh, thank you," Hamada-san said. "But I'm sorry to trouble you. Honestly, I'm not too bad off. But I apologize for not being able to make our appointment today."

Hamada-san looked a bit tired and pale to Eri, but his voice was strong. She sat on the sofa and noticed an expansive bookshelf that lined the room.

"So many books," Eri said.

"Oh, yes. We own a small bookstore here in Kanda. My nephew runs it."

The living room was awash in clutter. Papers, pens, notebooks and magazines covered a small desk in the corner with a computer and an oversized leather chair that didn't seem to match. An armoire held a large collection of English-style china, plates, bowls and cups piled on top of each other every which way. The dog's plaid, rumpled bed sat in another corner, several squeaky toys scattered nearby along with a leash and a harness and a magazine about dog training opened face down on the floor. A pile of newspapers sat askew near the entryway near a backpack bulging at the seams propped up against a wall next to a broom and a dustbin. A coat rack that had seen better days held an assortment of sweaters and sweatshirts, and a variety of potted plants—ferns and the like—constituting almost a mini jungle, were placed in rows next to a portable television, a watering can and a garden gnome.

The dog gave a small bark. "This is Nana-chan," Hamada-san said.

"She's so cute," Eri said.

Hajime arrived with a tray holding a teapot and cups and a ceramic plate where he placed the cream puffs.

"Why not sit at the kotatsu," he said and the two of them sat on the floor with Hamada-san and the dog, warming their legs by the heater under the blanket attached to the table.

Eri sipped her tea and nibbled on her cream puff. They talked about the family bookstore and Eri's job, her trips to Disneyland, and a *ryokan* in Kyoto Hajime had stayed at recently for research for an article for his magazine. They ordered sushi from a local restaurant that delivered and ate dinner together at the kotatsu. It all felt so natural, so easy.

Around eight o'clock Eri said that she needed to get back home, though she was just being polite; she could have stayed much longer. She wished Hamada-san well and Hajime walked her to the door.

"Thank you for your concern about my father," he said.

She slipped into her shoes and they shook hands. Hajime held on to her hand a little longer than necessary and smiled. But it didn't feel too forward. In fact, it felt just right. Eri looked into his face and he smiled again and she smiled too. He invited her to come over the following Sunday, as if it were the most natural thing in the world, and she said yes.

And then she realized there was something else. It was both a new and a familiar feeling.

A spark of joy.

SUITE FOR THE LADY IN RED

by Suanne Schafer

Langley, Virginia, 24 February 2013

"Eliminate her, Mark."

My ulcer began a slow burn as soon as Caulder gave me the assignment. I ignored the pain. He'd interpret any reaction as a sign of weakness.

Caulder had joined the CIA in 1985. A couple years later, I mustered in. I'd been active military in a clandestine DCS outfit longer than he'd been CIA. Bottom-line—who had actual seniority? Back in 2008, we were candidates for the same promotion. He took credit for my breakthrough in a tough assignment and yanked the position from under my nose. I'd been treading water since, trying to survive until retirement. Our professional relationship remained strained. Our friendship ended.

Five years ago, Caulder had recruited the target, Sarah Griffon. I knew her by reputation only.

"What's your theory?" I asked.

"Sarah, uh, Dr. Griffon, came to see me three months ago, wanting out, begging to be released." His eyes darted toward me, then away. "Wouldn't give a reason. Said it was personal. For Christ's sake, I couldn't let her go. We'd spent months embedding her in the Fatah al-Islam refugee camp. She'd successfully seduced Baroodi. He was beginning to trust her."

His fingernails drummed on his desk, irritating the hell out of me.

"Why take her out? Everyone's entitled to some time off."

Caulder stood and paced. "Damn it. I told her she could go when she completed this assignment. Said she couldn't wait. Then disappeared."

I took Griffon's dossier from Caulder's extended hand. As I scanned the pages, I raised my eyebrows. Sarah Griffon. Born Arlington, Virginia, June 16, 1983. Unlike me, she had an enviable pedigree. Her father, a career diplomat, was a handsome blend of wealthy white Anglo-Saxon Protestant and French-Moroccan. Her Lebanese mother was a world-renowned cellist. Griffon spoke half a dozen languages. The only thing we had in common was classical guitar.

Rather than compete with her illustrious parents, she attended medical school. A respected physician, her forthright stance on human rights and her work with Doctors Without Borders put her at the forefront of international political debates. Her patrician background allowed her to hobnob with world-class movers and shakers. With her medical credentials, she easily accessed places the organization couldn't, such as refugee camps where terrorists bred like mosquitoes.

Caulder, recognizing both her potential and her connections, had pulled her into the fold. After training her personally, he used her for hand-picked missions, which she carried out with aplomb. Some stateside staff resented the fact that Griffon got the plum assignments, leading to rumors of a quid pro quo sexual relationship between Caulder and Griffon. I didn't doubt the rumors. Though they remained unsubstantiated, the scuttlebutt continued, spread by office-bound assholes who had no fucking idea how difficult Middle Eastern missions could be. Often the only clue to whether you faced friend or foe was how a man draped his keffiye.

As proud of his protégée's meteoric rise as if he'd hatched her himself, Caulder had obviously taken her defection quite personally.

I passed her documents back to him.

He sat down again. After extending a photograph to me, his fingers resumed their staccato percussion on his desk. "This is the first time she's been seen since she vanished."

I sucked in a breath, staring at the close-up long after memorizing the image. A woman to die for. Black curls. Olive skin. Luscious lips.

I got lost in her chocolate eyes. Seconds passed before I remembered to exhale.

"She is lovely, isn't she?" Caulder's voice betrayed his emotion though his face remained expressionless.

I nodded, though in my opinion, good spies preferred anonymity. Like me. Gray hair, gray eyes, unremarkable features. Griffon's beauty and outspokenness made her unforgettable.

He tossed me the next photo as if the paper were too hot to handle.

The second I picked it up, I knew why. Looking like an illustration from the *Sports Illustrated* swimsuit issue, Griffon walked on a beach hand in hand with a man I vaguely recognized. Her hair was wild and tangled by the wind, her face luminous. A tiny bikini top barely covered perfect breasts. A damp sarong clung like plastic wrap to her hips revealing parts of a female I hadn't seen in years.

Clearly Caulder had the hots for the woman. Hell, who wouldn't? Just looking at her image, I was half in love with her myself.

"Who's the guy?" I handed the photos back to Caulder.

"Ariel Chabat. Some kind of musician."

No wonder he seemed familiar. Not just any performer. A virtuoso. The best classical guitarist in the world. I had a couple of his CDs at home.

"He's a Spanish Jew. A real Zionist. Moved to Tel Aviv six years ago." Caulder growled his irritation. "By consorting with him, Sarah's undermined everything we've accomplished in the Gaza Strip."

"She's probably in love."

Caulder snorted. "She knows better. We all do. When was the last time you let a woman interfere with your duty?" He stopped short. His gaze flicked to mine and then away. "Sorry, Mark. I didn't mean—"

I waved my hand to cut him off. I knew where he was heading with that remark and had no desire to go there. "Why me?"

"You're our most experienced operative."

"You've been around longer," I countered.

He shook his head. "Can't be objective. I trained her."

"You mean you fucked her."

Caulder stood before his office window staring out at the compound. He turned and gave me a nasty look, suggesting I'd overstep my bounds. "I wish." He snorted. "Hey, I retire July one. Karen's planning a second honeymoon. She'd kill me if I took off now hunting for a woman half my age."

"Where's Griffon now?"

"Chabat performs with the Madrid symphony orchestra the nineteenth. We think she'll be there."

I sat upright. "That's tomorrow."

"Short notice, I know. We can't let her vanish again." Caulder swallowed hard and looked down, avoiding my gaze.

As I witnessed his discomfort, I doubted he'd told the truth about not fucking Griffon. In the past, he'd had more than one May-December affair, but never with such a gorgeous woman. If he had any feelings for Griffon at all, how he could he have ordered her to seduce Baroodi? I decided a man who'd screw his best friend out of a job wouldn't think twice about sending a woman he loved into harm's way.

While Caulder seemed sufficiently virile to keep two women happy, I suspected Karen finally put her foot down about his philandering.

He stopped pacing long enough to pull a packet from a desk drawer and pitch it to me.

I snatched it in midair. My name, Mark Kuhlmeier, had been scrawled across the envelope with a thick black marker. I ran my finger under the flap and removed Spanish and French passports, train and plane tickets, an employee ID for the Auditorio Nacional de Music and a fat stack of Euros.

Caulder stuck out his hand, terminating our little chat. "Take her out, Mark. She's a loose cannon."

I gave him a lukewarm shake.

Over the past thirty years, I'd brought down dozens of enemies but really didn't like killing. Taking out one of our own rankled me. Somehow, I'd bet this assignment had more to do with Caulder placating his wife than Griffon's defection.

On the overnight flight to Madrid, I drifted into an uneasy sleep in which memories of Judith resurfaced. Nightmares I'd thought long buried had been stirred up by Caulder's comment.

Tel Aviv, December 27, 2008

A steaming cup of coffee in one hand, Judith opened the door to the balcony with the other. Still wet from sex, clad only in love, her belly rounded with our child, she stood outside watching the morning traffic in Tel Aviv.

"Call in sick," I begged.

"I can't. There's a war going on."

"Come inside. Someone will see you."

"You just want to have your way with me again." She turned to watch me dress and laughed. "Going commando?"

I ignored her as I tugged my jeans up my thighs, focused on getting the zipper over my latest hard-on.

Crash! Something shattered on the floor. Shards of coffee cup skittered across the terrazzo -as a whine passed my ear.

Surprised, I looked up.

Judith's mouth opened several times. She staggered, took one step and collapsed to her knees. Blood pumped from her chest, a massive hole where her left breast used to be. A bullet whizzed past my shoulder. I dropped to the floor and crawled toward her. Another round zipped by me and embedded in the wall. The next struck Judith in the back of the head. Bits of brain and droplets of blood splattered me and the walls of her apartment.

I stood and raced to the balcony railing. Across the parking lot, a man, features hidden by a baseball cap, dropped from the roof of the building to a nearby tree, then to the ground. Knowing I moved too slowly, I ran to the bedroom. Last night I'd been so eager to get Judith into bed that I hadn't put my firearm in its usual place. Valuable seconds passed as I dug through discarded clothing and rumpled sheets to retrieve it. By the time I raced barefooted down the stairs to street level, the assassin was gone.

As always, I woke up at that point, sweating, out of breath, heart racing, regretting my inability to save the woman I loved—or avenge her.

Since Judith's death, I'd been celibate. And impotent. After seven years of self-imposed abstinence, I doubted the old dog would ever rise again.

Madrid, 25 February 2013

The next morning, I wandered up the Calle del Príncipe de Vergara to the auditorium. With a point-and-shoot camera around my neck, a *Fodor's Guide* in one hand and a worn backpack, I followed a docent through the concert hall, listening to him lecture in badly-accented French.

My Madrid contact, "Emilio" according to his name tag, caught up with me in the toilet. We pissed in unison. The roar of our streams drowned out our whispered conversation.

He said, "I tracked Chabat to the Hotel Ritz. No one's seen Griffon yet. He's ordered dozens of roses and an elegant dinner for after his performance tonight. So either she's coming in, or he's got himself some fancy whore."

"It's her." Only true love could drag a woman like Griffon out of hiding.

Emilio and I exited separately. I continued my reconnaissance while he disappeared backstage.

When the tour ended, I exited with the other tourists. I found the main concert hall, the Sala Sinfónica, perfect for my needs. Twenty-two hundred seats circled the stage except upstage which was occupied by a large pipe organ. There were no dark wings with heavy curtains Griffon could hide behind while enjoying her lover's performance. Anywhere she sat she'd be visible. From the catwalk above the nosebleed seats, I'd get a clean shot.

Hours before the concert, I swiped my ID into the auditorium's card reader and walked in like I belonged. Dressed in the gray coveralls of an electrician, I climbed to the catwalk. Security would be tighter at the time of the performance, so I smuggled my weapon in early. Pretending to adjust lights, I duct taped my Colt to the underside of a lamp housing. Minutes later, in the bowels of the auditorium, I snagged a janitor's pushcart. With broom and dust rag in hand, I checked out Chabat's dressing room. Then I wandered around with the cart, keeping busy enough to avoid second-guessing the project.

Show time approached. From stage left I watched for Griffon as the seats filled. I'd begun to think Caulder's intelligence was faulty when, at the last minute, she appeared. Dressed in a scarlet gown, she sat front row dead center. She couldn't have made herself a more obvious target.

In the first half of his program, Chabat, accompanied by the orchestra, worked his way through an astonishing repertoire, highlighting two centuries of works for guitar. Under the spell of the music, I relaxed.

Patrons mingled during intermission while the stagehands cleared the orchestra's chairs preparing for Chabat's solo pieces. As I moved toward the catwalk, my right foot hit something slick. I slipped and nearly fell. I looked down to investigate. Someone had dropped a program. Without bothering to look at it, I picked it up and stuck it beneath my overalls into my shirt to read later.

In the catwalk, crouching low to avoid being seen, I pulled the Colt free from its tape, attached the suppressor, then slid the pistol into the voluminous pocket of my uniform. The cartridges, DRT frangible hollow points, contained a compressed powder that disintegrated into a fine dust when they struck a target, causing massive internal damage. One shot should take out Griffon without passing through her to harm innocent bystanders. The final explosion of clapping just before Chabat's encore would mask the report of my firearm.

The second half of the performance included Chabat's exquisite rendering of Tárrega's Recuerdos de la Alhambra. The piece always jerked my heartstrings and suited my melancholy mood.

God, I envied Chabat's skill. With more bravado than talent, I'd played guitar in high school and college. Peer pressure made me hide my love for classical music by cranking out rock and roll on a beat-up Stratocaster. Years had passed since I'd plunked out a tune. Maybe I'd take up playing again when I retired—if I lived that long.

Thunder shook the theater. The audience stood, clapping wildly. "Bravissimo!" and "Encore!" echoed off the rafters.

Shit! The sudden burst of noise jerked me back to the moment. I'd gotten lost in the music long enough to jeopardize the assignment. I refocused. My fifty-six-year-old knees creaked as I knelt on the catwalk. Obscured by the brilliant stage lights, I slid the forty-five from my pocket, flipped off the safety and made sure a round was in the chamber. After popping a couple of Tums to calm the fire in my gut, I took a deep breath, steadied my hand against the railing—and waited.

Ignoring two thousand people, Chabat played for Griffon alone. Mesmerized by his performance, she blew him a kiss at the end of one spectacular number. Neither her affair with Caulder nor her seduction of Baroody could compare with the obvious chemistry between her and Chabat. No wonder she wanted out.

After Chabat's final note reverberated into nothingness, he stood, leaned his guitar on the edge of his seat and bowed elegantly. Behind him, stagehands brought in another chair, foot rest and a second instrument still in its case.

He swiped long fingers through wavy brown hair, stepped to stage front, bent toward Griffon and motioned for her to join him.

A demure Griffon stood but held back.

Chabat wiggled his fingers again, cajoling her.

People in adjacent seats playfully pushed her forward.

Griffon's lover took her hands and lifted her onto the apron. After a fierce kiss, Chabat wrapped one arm around her and said to the audience, "¡*Mira!* Look, everyone. We got married today." He raised her left hand and flashed her ring to the audience. The patrons responded with louder applause accompanied by whistles and cheers.

Chabat strutted with manly pride. Griffon glowed.

Fuck. I would have to take her out on her wedding day. I couldn't do it. I started to walk away, but Caulder's voice echoed in my head. When was the last time you let a woman interfere with your duty?

I turned back, rubbed my burning gut, and wondered why Griffon had worn red.

Chabat tucked a curl behind his wife's ear, revealing a delicate pink shell. He had unknowingly cleared my target for me, but something in the way he'd caressed her stole my breath. To block his gesture from my mind, I closed my eyes, refocused on the job at hand, and inhaled deeply. When I opened my eyes, I raised the pistol until the laser sight kissed Griffon's right ear, and exhaled.

As I squeezed the trigger, Chabat swept Griffon off her feet and swung her in a joyous twirl. The bullet entered the back of his head. Instant kill. Wrong person. Major fuck-up.

Like a Rube Goldberg contraption, Chabat tilted into Griffon in slow motion, knocking her backwards. She stumbled into his instrument. Stepped on it. Dissonant notes ripped the air. Her high heels tangled in guitar strings. She crashed into his chair. He fell on her. Her anguished scream soared above the noise of the spectators.

Instantly silent, the stunned audience was paralyzed.

Griffon lay on her back beneath him, calling his name, begging someone to help him, frantically trying to lift him off her as his blood poured out. A haphazard pile of chairs, instrument stands and sheet music partially obscured my view of her. I could still see the desperate waving of her reddened hands. The debris didn't block her screams.

Seconds later, the crowd went berserk. People leaped on the stage to assist her.

Too many spectators surrounded her. I couldn't get a clear shot anymore.

Now fully aware of what had happened, the onlookers began scanning the auditorium trying to figure out where the attack had originated.

Taking advantage of the ensuing pandemonium, I escaped before anyone saw me.

On the Calle, I hopped on the first bus leaving the area. Half an hour later, in the bus station toilet, I tore off the coveralls and stuffed them in my knapsack along with the Colt and name tag.

Slipping out a different door, I grabbed a taxi to the train station. There I placed the backpack in a locker. Minutes later I entered the men's room and dropped the key into the tank of the second toilet on the left. Emilio would recover everything in a few days.

With seconds to spare before its departure, I caught the overnight train to Paris.

Paris, 26 February 2013

By the time I reached the City of Light, morning editions of *Le Monde*, *Le Figaro*, and the *International Herald Tribune* had made their way to the Gare d'Austerlitz station. I picked up the *Trib* and read it while taxiing to Charles de Gaulle airport.

Chabat was dead. No shit. I'd killed an international treasure. And destroyed a $60,000 Hermann Hauser guitar. Griffon survived but remained hospitalized mourning the dual loss of her husband and her unborn child. Double fuck.

I tossed the newspaper in the garbage and entered the departures terminal at de Gaulle. When I presented my passport to buy a ticket to D.C., I discovered the playbill I'd picked up in the Madrid auditorium. Tucked inside the booklet, an errata page revealed Chabat had changed his program at the last minute. He planned to premier his newest composition, *Suite for the Lady in Red.* Griffon would have made her musical debut in his duet for two guitars.

Langley, February 27, 2013

Caulder's secretary said, "Go on in," but I stopped outside his office and swallowed a few antacids before knocking.

"It's open." His voice penetrated the oak veneer door.

I entered.

He stared out the windows of his corner office, his back toward me, but pivoted the second my foot stepped on his carpet.

"Mark, what the fuck happened?"

The room crackled with tension, his and mine.

"Circumstances beyond my control." Despite the Tums, acid chewed my stomach. Seemed like it never stopped anymore.

"The collateral damage was too great," Caulder said. "You fucking took out an innocent bystander. The State Department is up in arms."

"You ordered it."

"I expected you of all people to be competent."

I dug my fist into my smoldering abdomen. "Caulder—"

He interrupted me, slamming his fist on his desk. "Ambassador Griffon moved Sarah from Madrid to some ritzy convalescent hospital in Switzerland. He's hired the Swiss-Security Agency to guard his daughter around the clock. Find her. Take her out."

In my cubicle, I scanned international news reports. In the Middle East, tensions had escalated to the boiling point. Ambassador Griffon blamed Baroodi, his daughter's ex-lover. Israel attributed Chabat's death to Hezbollah. The United States pointed its finger at the PLO. Baroodi held the U. S. responsible, claiming Griffon had been a spy, a Mata Hari sent to seduce him.

When I arrived in Bern the next morning, I found no trace of Griffon. Once again, she'd vanished. The Ambassador held the Swiss police and Swi-Sec responsible for her disappearance. But I knew she was a woman who didn't want to be found.

Langley, 30 April 2013

For two months, as I followed every conceivable lead, Caulder grew nastier, fuming constantly about my incompetence.

"What the fuck have you been doing with your time?" he bellowed. "Do you have any idea the flack the department will take, that I will take, if it comes out we killed a guitar player while trying to dispatch an ambassador's daughter? I'm not letting you jeopardize my reputation—or my retirement."

"It's not my fault. You taught her every trick she knows."

"She switched sides, Mark. This is a simple targeted killing."

In training we learned that assassination equaled murder. The U.S. Government did not condone the killing of someone who disagreed with policy. On the other hand, a "targeted kill" was more akin to self-defense in advance than murder. In Caulder's mind, Sarah had become an enemy combatant and fair game.

"You're letting the fact that she's a woman cloud your judgment." Caulder's voice seethed with venom. "This all harks back to Judith. Do I need to put someone else on the case?"

I shook my head. "I can handle it. Just a little more time."

"One month. I plan to retire with a clean slate."

Back in my cubicle, I searched my desk for another roll of antacids. That bastard would bring up Judith again.

Dragging my thoughts from the past, I stared at the photos in Griffon's file. Recently I'd spent so much time staring at her picture I felt I knew her. I no longer called her "Griffon." She'd become "Sarah." At night I'd wake up drenched in sweat, tormented by a recurrent dream in which Judith had Sarah's curls and wore a red dress, stained darker with the blood of husband and baby.

The burn in my belly grew to a steady blaze antacids couldn't touch.

In the end, I found Sarah by chance.

Some stupid college kid, returning from a summer slumming in Europe, got caught smuggling a kilo of hashish into New York's JFK. The Feds ran the photos on his digital camera through their facial recognition software. He'd snapped an image of a beautiful woman eating *tapas* at a Spanish cafe. Our missing agent. I traced her to the *Realejo Barrio*, the old Jewish quarter of Granada.

Sarah and I had never met, so I didn't bother with a disguise. Over the past several months I'd let my temples silver and allowed a beard to proliferate, which I trimmed to a neat goatee. I projected the persona of a middle-aged man going through a midlife crisis. The role suited me.

Granada, 14 May 2013. D minus 16 days

The first few days in Granada, I stayed in a hostel near the cafe where Sarah had been photographed. Every day I ate there, hoping she'd return. When she did, like a lovesick pup, I followed her up a steep hill to her home. A sign on her front door advertised a room for rent. I smiled. Things were finally looking up.

I easily charmed the landlady, a frail, black-garbed grandmother, with dollars, if not my rakish grin. She introduced herself as *Señora* Chabat.

A chill climbed my spine. "Are you—"

Before I finished the question, tears trailed down her cheeks. With a lace handkerchief, she dabbed her eyes. "Ariel was my great-grandson."

Fuck. I added her to my expanding list of casualties.

The *Señora* patted my hand. "I'm ninety-seven years old. Death and I are good friends. We become more intimate every day."

She gave me the keys and sent me upstairs to check out the apartment alone. Though her villa was elegant on the outside, the upper floor had been converted to four pieds-à-terre with thin walls and cheap furnishings.

I climbed the stairs to a tiny foyer, turned the key in the door on the left and walked in. Fair-sized living area. Adequate bedroom. Microscopic bath. Past those, a kitchenette with French doors. I opened the doors and stepped onto a balcony furnished with a bistro table, two chairs, a chaise lounge and a breathtaking, unobstructed view of the city. Mid-rise buildings squatted in prayer beneath the distant cathedral. A pair of louvered shutters divided my half-balcony from Sarah's. I unlatched them and crossed into her territory. Her outdoor space had identical furniture. I peeked through her windows. Her place mirrored mine.

Quickly I descended the steps and told the *Señora* I'd take the room. Then, staked out next door to Sarah, I awaited the perfect opportunity to win her confidence.

Every night before Caulder went to bed, he texted me with the number of days I had left to accomplish my mission. D minus nineteen days, D minus eighteen days, D minus seventeen days…I wondered if Karen actually reminded him to text me or if the act of crawling into bed with his wife stimulated a knee-jerk reaction.

Over several days, I familiarized myself with Sarah's routine. She cared for the *Señora* with genuine affection and ran the house with military precision. After breakfast, she left for the market with a basket on one arm to do the daily shopping.

At the morning and mid-afternoon meals we tenants shared with our landlady, I watched Sarah. The simple acts of eating, drinking, and conversing together lulled me into a sense of domesticity I hadn't known since Judith.

Once I could predict how long Sarah might be gone on her errands, I picked the lock on her door, slipped on vinyl gloves and snooped.

Not much in the living area. A utilitarian sofa. No phone to tap. No radio. No television. A black leather bag sat by at the front door, filled with her stethoscope and medical paraphernalia. A guitar lounged against the wall. I opened the case and groaned with lust. A Ramirez. As good as the Herman Hauser ruined when I killed

Chabat. I ran my fingers over the strings. Badly out of tune, the guitar hadn't been played recently. I wondered if the instrument was Chabat's or Sarah's. Next to the guitar, a CD player.

The bedroom didn't yield much either. Books in three languages. Lacy underwear stowed in a drawer made my heart race. The armoire held three pairs of jeans. Six T-shirts. One black dress. When I stroked the length of her silky white nightgown, I shivered.

Beyond learning Sarah's favorite toothpaste and soap, the bathroom gave up only her fragrance, Azahar. With a twist of the lid, I opened the bottle. The smell of orange blossoms spiraled through the air. I envisioned Sarah touching the golden perfume on her wrists, the pulse of her neck, then swallowed as I thought of the scent lying between her breasts. I always knew when she'd been on the stairs that led to our rooms, the aroma lingered there laced with her ever-present sadness.

After placing a couple of discrete bugs, I slipped back to my own apartment.

At night the sounds of her toilette penetrated our thin shared wall.

I felt a peculiar intimacy with her then, imagining being married to her, sharing a bedtime routine and sleeping spooned together after love-making. As she prepared for bed, she hummed a wistful tune I didn't recognize. Like *Recuerdos de la Alhambra*, its poignant notes made me long for something I couldn't name.

D minus fourteen days. Two weeks left. Despite Caulder's order to eliminate her, I still hadn't killed Sarah, though I could have taken her out at any time. By now, she and Judith were so twisted together in my head, I knew if I killed Sarah, I'd be no different than Judith's assassin.

Granada, 29 May 2013, D minus 1

A week later, at lunch, the *Señora* said, "Sarah, perhaps one of our guests might escort you to the concert tonight."

The old woman appraised each of us tenants before her eyes settled on me.

Realizing I'd been "volunteered," I said, "I'd be happy to." I understood the woman's logic. Her Sarah would be safe with an old man.

"*Abuela*, are you ill?" Sarah knelt before the Señora, immediately taking her pulse.

Señora Chabat protested as Sarah fussed over her. "Dear girl, I'm fine. I simply fear the evening will be too stressful for me."

"I understand." Sarah kissed the old woman's wrinkled cheek.

At 7:15, Sarah descended the stairs, wearing the black dress from her closet, a *mantilla* draped over her shoulder. Her ringlets, precariously pinned with chopsticks, would tumble like a house of cards were one chopstick removed. She was stunning but pale and taut with tension.

As I helped Sarah out of the taxi, the poster for the event caught my eye. Fuck. A musical tribute to Ariel Chabat featuring guitarists from around the world. My head swiveled searching for an escape route.

Sarah noticed. "*Abuela* didn't tell you?" With an apologetic shrug, she added, "Classical guitar isn't everyone's cup of tea."

"It's fine. I'll enjoy it."

"I hate this sort of thing." She grimaced. "But Ari was my husband. I have to stay. You don't."

"The *Señora* would be upset if I left you alone."

She shrugged.

Inside, Sarah listened to the performances, facing dead ahead, her hands so tightly clasped in her lap that her knuckles bleached. Her closed eyes dammed tears threatening to spill.

I knew the moment the music reached through her sorrow. She leaned back in her seat. Her hands relaxed and separated, her fingers twitched, then flew, playing the intricate notes on an imaginary guitar.

Afterwards, audience members and performers gathered around Sarah, acknowledging Chabat's extraordinary talent.

Someone called Sarah's name.

The crowd parted for an ancient gnome.

"Maestro." She greeted him with kisses on each cheek followed by a warm embrace.

He patted her hand. Tears streamed down his cheeks. "Ari was like a son—"

"I know." Her lips trembled. Her dammed tears overflowed. With the touch of a finger she captured a droplet and transferred it to the old man's cheek, blending their sorrow. "We share every tear."

When he tottered away, Sarah clutched my arm. Wild-eyed and trembling, she said, "I've got to leave!" At a near run, she dragged me out of the theater.

In silence we climbed the long hill back to the Chabat villa, Sarah a step or two ahead of me. Though the evening was muggy and warm, she wore the mantilla as tightly wound around her as her sorrow.

At the top of our stairs, she leaned her forehead against her door, her eyes so full of tears she couldn't insert the key into the lock.

"Allow me," I said, taking the keys from her hand. For a brief instant, she leaned into me and rested her head on my chest, seeking comfort. I wanted to taste her hair. Her Azahar swirled around me. With a deep breath, I wrapped my arms around her.

She pulled away.

"You could use a drink." I held the door for her. "I have a bottle of sherry, but no glasses."

She shook her head. "Thanks anyway." She half-smiled. "But I can lend you a glass."

"Don't make me drink alone."

Her lips twitched in surrender.

I dashed across the hall, found the bottle and returned to her apartment.

She handed me glasses. I poured the sherry.

"Give me a minute." She returned to the kitchen. "I'll put together tapas."

Over the tinkle of cutlery and plates I heard her humming that haunting melody again.

I wandered the apartment until, unable to resist, I lifted the guitar from its case. After picking a few sour notes, I began tuning it.

"The high E is still flat," she observed as she came into the living area carrying a tray of olives, peppers, a sliced baguette, slivered ham and dried apricots. She settled on her sofa and pulled the chopsticks from her hair releasing a tangle of loose ringlets.

More than anything, I wanted to become entrapped in those curls. Instead, I kept tuning the instrument. "Do you play?"

She shook her head.

"I thought I'd be the next Eric Clapton when I was a teenager."

"007 for me." She grinned. After a pause, she added, "But I suppose, in reality, a spy's life isn't all that glamorous."

To change the subject, I ran my fingers over the guitar strings and asked, "What's that song you hum all the time? I can't place it."

She looked puzzled.

Damn. The tune was so ingrained in her, she wasn't aware she vocalized it.

"It goes like this." I played a dozen notes.

"No!" She burst into tears and ran into the bathroom.

For a few minutes, I waited to see if she'd come out. When her sobs showed no sign of subsiding, I chugged both our sherries, grabbed the bottle and retreated to my apartment.

The night remained muggy. I headed to the kitchen, dropped off the sherry and cracked the seal on the bourbon. I opened the French doors, praying for a breath of cool air. Sitting on the balcony, I started drinking straight out of the bottle. The first gulp burnt my esophagus, lit a fire in my gut, then settled into a golden glow. The alcohol left me maudlin, morose, and drunk enough to admit that I'd fallen in love with Sarah.

My cell vibrated. The daily text from Caulder. *D minus one. Eliminate the problem within twenty-four hours, or your career is over.*

Fuck him! With a flip of my wrist, I tossed the phone on the chaise then dropped down next to it.

I was screwed. If I didn't kill Sarah, Caulder would send someone else to do it. She'd be dead anyway, and my career would be kaput. If I did murder her, my life would be over. Double fuck. Suddenly, I wanted to screw up Caulder's life like he was fucking up mine. To make his retirement a living hell.

After a shower, I looked at myself in the mirror, noting the grizzled hair that surrounded my cock, the slack ball sac that dangled beneath. You're getting rather long in the tooth, Mark. I gave the old dog a stroke or two, but he didn't bother to rouse.

During the night, guitar music floated in from the balcony and awakened me. Sarah must have been too upset to sleep. The amber eye of the clock blinked 2:00 a.m. I stripped the sheet from the bed and carried it outside to the chaise. There, naked and half-asleep, I listened to Sarah play. At first, not having practiced in months, she fumbled, cursed and started over multiple times. Finally muscle memory returned, and she ran through several songs flawlessly.

The music changed to a recording of a lone guitar, a plaintive melody in A-minor, reminiscent of Sarah's tune. A man missing his lover.

Plink. Plink. Plink. With a shuddering sigh, Sarah tuned her instrument up a third before playing along with the recorded music, her guitar a woman replying tenderly to her man.

I recognized the tune Sarah always hummed.

Suddenly I realized I was hearing the duet Chabat wrote for their wedding, *Suite for the Lady in Red.* He had recorded his part so she could practice while they were apart.

In complex counterpoint, the two tremolo-laced melodies intertwined in the most intricate guitar piece I'd ever heard.

Sarah paused, then began the second movement where the joy of lovers reunited segued into what I could only call fuck-me music. The male guitar led with a pulsating bass, the female replied breathlessly. They climaxed together in a crescendo ending with simultaneous thumps on the soundboards of the instruments and a three beat pause. Afterglow followed, a series of descending arpeggios.

Finally, the third part in A-major reprised the opening but with a sweet, uplifting resolution.

I moved to the shutters, tilting the louvers so I could see Sarah. She sat on the chaise, instrument in her lap, replaying the second movement, her mouth open, her foot tapping like a metronome, her body responding to the thrusts of the male guitar.

In her white nightgown she looked pure. But, like me, she'd played the game. Like me, she'd followed orders. I bet she never told that new husband of hers what she did for a living. Never told him Caulder had fucked her. Never told him she'd fucked Baroodi.

Since Chabat's death, she'd drowned in misery. She needed someone to ease her pain. Someone with blood on their hands. Someone who understood what it was like to lose a lover and a child to an assassin. Someone who knew how living a double life could make you forget who you were. Someone who understood what it's like to whore yourself for your country. Someone to love her. Someone like me.

Before I could open the shutters to go to her, she stopped half way through the movement, laid her guitar on the floor, stood, walked across the balcony.

The recording continued, Chabat playing alone.

With her head bowed, Sarah leaned on the rail and peered at the city lights. For a moment, I thought she might jump, but with a sob, she ran both hands through her curls. Then she tilted her head back. Her fingers meandered down the front of her neck before arriving at her breasts. Her pelvis undulated to the throbbing of Chabat's guitar still playing on the CD. With a whimper, she pulled her gown off and threw it on the chaise.

My heart raced.

In the moonlight her olive skin seemed gilded.

Sarah turned from the balcony railing and restarted the second movement before sinking to the chaise, caressing herself, teasing her nipples into peaks.

Stunned, I adjusted the shutters for a better view, then inhaled sharply at the unfamiliar sensation of my cock stirring.

Watching Sarah, I grew harder. Painfully hard. Teenage boy hard.

As her fingers slipped past dense curls into the valley between her thighs, she moaned.

I reached for my cock, reveling in its power.

For the first time that night, a cool breeze stirred, carrying toward me the intoxicating fragrance of orange blossoms mixed with her desire.

Keeping time with Chabat's fuck-me music, her hand moved faster between her legs. Her breath grew ragged.

To keep from groaning, I bit my lip. Seven years of long-buried semen jetted into the shutters. I staggered with the intensity of the release.

"Yes, Ari!" she cried, arching her body with her orgasm.

My heart stopped. Seven years of waiting—and she called out for another man.

With my head resting against the louvers, I watched Sarah till her breathing slowed. Lying on her back, one arm curved upward, one beneath lush breasts, she slept. A satisfied smile graced succulent lips. Black curls cascaded over golden skin. Her body echoed the curves of the guitar on the ground beside her.

Seven years.

My abdomen tensed. My stomach blazed into an inferno. I went inside and grabbed the antacid bottle in the bathroom.

Two Tums, then four, didn't knock out the burn. Twelve Tums later, fire still raced up my esophagus. I tasted blood. Hell must taste like this.

Seven years, and she'd never be mine.

After retrieving my pistol from the nightstand, I opened the shutters and stepped toward Sarah. I looked down at her, then fired one shot into her heart.

"Ari," she breathed, then her body went limp.

Seven years, and her last breath carried another man's name.

Plink. Drip. Plink. Drip. Drops of her blood sounded the guitar strings before falling into its womb.

I sank onto the chaise and lifted Sarah's head to my lap. With my left hand, I twisted her curls like Chinese finger traps around my fingers, determined to bind us forever. With my right hand, I brought the Colt to my mouth. I swallowed the barrel and squeezed the trigger.

Originally published by Geminid Press, LLC, Albuquerque, NM in their *Night Lights* anthology.

ME AND GABRIEL

by Linda Moore

I had no business going to Colombia that year. The narco wars had escalated, increasing the body count of innocents who had been caught between Pablo Escobar's Medellín and the Cali cartels' battle over the lucrative drug trade.

Louis, the owner of a New York gallery, had invited our gallery to exhibit at Bogotá's new art fair, FIART. More established American gallerists had watched the carnage on the news and refused to participate. Our gallery was struggling, and a chance to connect to serious collectors with matching checkbooks convinced me we should take the risk.

"An art fair…in the most violent place on the planet?" My husband shouted the question and shook his head as he gestured toward our children, then ages eight and eleven.

I dove into the project with the energy and the resolve my dwindling bank balance demanded. The gallery staff invited collectors in that region to attend and pondered what art might interest Bogotanos, ultimately choosing to exhibit a series of paintings and encaustic boxes informed by Colombian Gabriel García Márquez's novel *One Hundred Years of Solitude.* Artist DeLoss McGraw had captured the color and energy of this Nobel Laureate's masterpiece.

Flipping through a decades-old paperback of *One Hundred Years of Solitude* to review passages in Spanish, a daydream emboldened me to invite García Márquez to visit FIART to view these artworks. The probability that he would come was low—okay, near zero--but in a venture permeated with magic realism, the irrational seems possible.

I wrote to the U.S. Cultural Attaché and convinced her to forward an invitation to Garcia-Marquez. He'd promised Colombian President Gaviria to co-host eight Latin American presidents at a summit that week and would not be able to attend.

The Chanel-meets-Bulgari crowd gathered at FIART's opening gala. A gauntlet of armed police positioned themselves like castle guards at the Fair's entrance, and it was clear they were not there to worry about jewel thieves.

The event had a congenial atmosphere with serious collectors purchasing works by Latin American artists, and Colombians intrigued by the settings and characters from *One Hundred Years,* like

'Macondo' and 'El coronel,' depicted in the paintings. We traded favorite lines from that old copy of the book I'd brought.

The next morning, a runner from the Art Fair office delivered a note: Call the United States Embassy immediately. Were we being evacuated? Was something wrong at home? The kids?

I rushed to the office and returned the call. The Cultural Attaché said García Márquez had called. He was coming to the Fair…that afternoon…with Colombian President César Gaviria.

I phoned California and told McGraw the news. In a voice that crackled over the antiquated lines, alarm inserted itself between the words.

He was elated one of his literary heroes would view his works that often pay tribute to such icons. "Give him one of the paintings," McGraw said.

"That's generous of you." I paused. "Wait. Which one?"

"You choose. You'll know."

Artists and families passed their Saturday afternoon wandering the aisles. I looked at my watch again and again. Suddenly, sirens sounded, and everyone rushed toward the main entrance. President Gaviria strolled in with an expensive-suited posse and nodded to the stunned art lovers.

Moments later, a roar, the type heard when a soccer goal is scored, vibrated against the roof. García Márquez entered and made his way through the crush of fans.

The lines on his face lifted the corners of his mouth into a smile. He ignored my trembling hand and leaned forward to kiss my cheeks.

We chatted about the ideas that inspired McGraw's wooden boxes covered with encaustic images depicting the characters and scenes of the novel. I removed one from the wall and showed him the text collaged on the back comparing his own sentences to Faulkner's. He studied the words, lifted his tortoise shell glasses to his forehead, and looked at me.

"What happens…" he said, "is that I forget what I write."

We laughed about how the literati poured every sentence searching for hidden meanings. This small painting of the quirky Coronel Buendía relaxing in a hammock rendered in colorful wax was the right choice.

I placed it into his soft hands. "The artist wants you to have this."

"*De verdad?* You're too kind." He turned it over to study the details on the front. "I want to do something for you. When are you leaving?" He searched the crowd for his assistant and waved him over. "We must do something for her."

I shook my head. "Your visit *is* a special gift for me."

He persisted, urging the assistant to come up with an idea.

I interrupted. "Maybe a small thing?" I reached for the old paperback and asked him to sign a yellowed page. I cringed after I'd said it because Garcia Marquez was known not to autograph books to avoid a horde with requests.

He took the book and ran his fingers over the tattered cover. He removed his glasses and looked into my eyes. "Where did you get this?"

His stern tone surprised me, and I babbled a response. "I bought it during my student days in Madrid when I donated blood to scrape together pesos for books and sangria. Sorry it's so worn."

He leaned forward and explained. "When the publisher sent this edition from Buenos Aires to Bogotá, the Colombian government impounded the shipment and destroyed the books." His eyes filled with sadness at the memory. "This is a rare copy."

I had no words.

He pulled a pen from his tweed jacket, drew a simple flower, and wrote, *Una flor para Linda -Gabriel.*

I left the exhibition hall that evening and returned to the hotel with the signed book that had been transformed into a treasure. Soldiers with machine guns guarded the entrance to the Tequendama Hotel where the Colombian military would imprison Escobar's wife and child, in what became a successful effort to lure him from his hiding place to his execution. I marched past the weapons with the book clutched to my chest like a shield.

SHATTERED CIRCA '72

by Robin Taylor

One summer night you're sitting next to a square jawed man on the sofa in your lovely living room with the shiny wood floors and Persian rugs.

As you listen to him quietly discussing the subject of fixing your car, you forget for a moment that he's your teacher, a Marine Biology professor at the local college where you hope to finish up your degree.

Tonight after class, your car refused to start and your teacher, just happening by, came to your rescue and gave it a jump. Afterwards, he followed you home, concerned that you might not make it all the way. He has no idea how grateful you are and always will be.

As the soon to be divorced mother of four, you have no time for car troubles and such. To express your appreciation, you invite him in for a drink.

Now, sitting side by side on the sofa, you sip red wine discussing the car and a good mechanic he knows. He has a nice smile and glistening eyes. Something about the man strikes you as charming and you begin to forget he's your teacher.

Your children are sleeping upstairs after a hard day of play and your husky, black lab, King, snores at your feet. The afternoon, fraught with tension about the car, has settled into a calm, pleasant night.

It's hard to believe you were standing before a Judge in a custody hearing before lunch. The children will stay with you. But, what if things had gone differently? Your hands tremble at the thought, so you shove them under your thighs to make them stop, reminding yourself that the bad days will be behind you soon. You lean back into the sofa, allow yourself to relax and listen to the man as he tells stories and even makes you laugh, something you haven't done in a while.

You'll be divorced in a month. Your ten-year-old daughter thinks you're to blame. Sometimes *you* think you're to blame. Maybe, if you'd been prettier, less needy, or…? She doesn't know about her daddy's drinking, the cheating, how he hits you with the butt of his gun…always in the stomach so no one can see the bruises. She has no idea how many times you've stopped him from beating her for not practicing the piano. Luckily, those days are over. You hope.

"Professor Harris, I'm so thankful for your help tonight. You have no idea how much."

"Please, call me Tim. Glad I could help. Mom raised us on her own. I know how hard it can be. Certainly don't want your car giving out on you with four children to cart around, now do you?"

"No, no. Not having the car would be awful. We're going through… um, I'm getting a divorce, Tim."

The teacher nods and glances at your hand. There's a white circle of skin on your tanned finger where you once wore your wedding band. Your eyes well up. You bite your lip.

"I assumed that was the case," he says. "He's crazy to let you go."

"Are you married?"

"Not for a long time. She lives with her mother in Daytona."

"I'm sorry."

"Don't be. We were never happy. Grew apart, I guess. She gave me Mike, though. Something to be said for that. What about you two?"

Your stomach tightens.

"Sort of like your situation, I suppose."

"Guess we're just two peas in a pod…"

You nod. He'd probably croak if he knew the truth.

You study his face. You like the way the skin crinkles up around his eyes when he smiles. King stirs at your feet. You scratch his ears and feel lighter, although you're not sure why. The teacher sips his wine. You talk about things that don't matter. It feels nice.

After a while, you kick off your shoes and when he tells you a joke about Nixon and his five-o'clock shadow, you laugh so hard you almost spit out your wine. Caught up in the moment, he pats your knee. For a brief second, the two of you stare at his hand. He blushes and yanks it away.

"I'm so sorry!"

"It's okay, Tim. It's fine, really it is."

It's the first time another man's touched you since you were twenty, but you keep that to yourself. As he tries to recover, you tell him about the first kiss you stole when you were five and how the object of your affection, first-grader Henry Alstead, told the teacher you'd branded him like a cow with your mouth. The story puts the teacher at ease, and he slaps his own knee and chuckles. Once the moment is passed, he tells you about his latest snorkeling trip to the Keys and his son, Mike, who recently went missing in Viet Nam.

Lulled by the comfort of the moment, you're startled a bit, when King begins to twitch and jumps up. Smiling, you listen to the man, but watch your dog, pacing and sniffing the air. You wonder what's gotten his attention. The only sound in the room, besides your own breathing, is the teacher's deep voice, which goes silent when King's fur bristles and he suddenly begins to alert. Ears pricked, body rigid, he starts to circle, sniffing the air. Then he stops in the center of the room, his eyes fixed on the French doors that lead from the living room to the front door.

No longer concerned with the teacher, you move to King's side in a flash. Hot tension from his body flows into your flesh when you rest your hand on his back. Following his gaze, you startle when a low, menacing growl begins to rumble down deep in his throat. Oddly, as quickly as it starts, it stops. He looks up at you, cocks his head sideways and releases a high-pitched whine. It pierces the silence in the room. You don't know what this sound means. He's never made it before.

You rub his back, whisper into his neck, "It's alright. It's alright," but your voice betrays you when it cracks. The whine turns to a whimper-then disappears. You and the teacher exchange a glance. King's attention returns to the doors. He positions his body in front of yours. His upper lip curls back, he growls, bares his teeth.

Then you see.

An ominous blackness takes hold of your senses. King snarls. The teacher stands, plants his feet, clenches his fists. He's seen combat before.

Within seconds, the French doors burst open, and a man appears. It's your soon to be ex-husband, the father of your children, the man you once loved.

He's muttering and shouting, waving a gun.

The teacher yells, "Down!" King whimpers. You notice a picture of you, your husband, and your children, hanging on the wall across the room. You're all dressed in your Sunday best. Your husband is holding your hand.

Now he's holding a sawed-off shotgun, and he's pointing it right at your face. Spittle spews from his mouth when he shouts your name and other things you can't quite make out. Every hair on your body stands on end, and for a brief instant, the whole room seems to sway. King is snapping and barking. An otherworldly power propels your forward just like it did the night he punched your swollen belly when you were pregnant with Rusty. He's not going to hurt you again.

You lunge at him, smacking the gun barrel aside with your hand. A deadly spray of bullets is unleashed. They sing past the side of your head, barely missing your face, their song, a hateful siren to your ear. They splinter the walls and the floors. The force of the shot sends your husband stumbling backwards. The teacher wrestles him to the ground.

Burnt smoke fills the room, scratching your throat and clogging your nose. White gun powder floats in the air before landing on all of you, like a dusting of powdered sugar.

Struggling against the weight of the teacher, your husband moans in pain and swears at the top of his lungs. There is blood splatter on your arms, but it's not from you. The rifle butt exploded into your husband's forearm. His trigger hand looks like raw meat. He grabs it and screams.

The teacher frisks him, discovering two loaded pistols tucked in the pockets of his Burberry coat. "Looks like he was coming for all of you," he says, as he gently pushes the pistols across the floor, out of your husband's reach.

You stand in a daze, unable to move, wondering if a person can live without a face. The teacher orders you to grab the shotgun, call the police, get help from the neighbor next door. The raging blast of the gun exploding still rings in your ears, and gets mixed up with the voice of your teacher and your husband's pathetic wailing. Just then, a new sound enters the room. Through the jumble of noise, the whimper of a child's voice cries, "Daddy! Daddy! Daddy!"

Your stomach twists when your little girl stumbles through the swirling haze of smoke. She looks so small and helpless in her flowing white nightgown with its big pink bow. You stare in horror as her eyes take in the sight of her bloody father struggling to escape the clutches of a strange man, and her mother standing nearby, frozen, a shotgun dangling by her side.

That's when your heart swells with pain more than fear.

How much did she see? What did she see? You want to tell her it's not what it seems. I didn't shoot your father, I swear. You need to explain what's happened, but how? For a brief second confusion clouds her eyes, then she shoots you an accusatory look before consoling her father. You try to warn her, be careful of him, don't get too close…but you can't make any sound come out of your mouth.

A crushing sensation seizes your heart.

You have to get her out of the room. You take a step forward and almost trip. Something is blocking your way. When you realize King's lifeless body lies at your feet, you drop to your knees. Rivers of blood stream from his head, some of it seeps into the edge of your skirt. Silent tears gush from your eyes. You bury your face in the singed fur of his neck, wishing you'd ignored the Vet and fixed him a steak, just once.

The teacher urges you to please get some help, only this time his voice is tender and soft. You want to crawl into his arms so he can shield you from what's happened and what's to come.

Rusty calls out your name and for a second, you think that surely you've been transported to hell. The silhouette of his little body, clad in his batman pajamas and cape, appears in the doorway, back-lit by the living room lamp. He's rubbing his eyes with his tiny fists. You leap to your feet, take his hand, and rush him past his moaning father, his dead dog, his whimpering sister and the teacher, who just stopped in for a friendly drink.

Using your body as a shield from the sight of his family in ruin, you get him out of the house, into the fresh evening air. Usually crickets are chirping their innocent hymns to the stars, but not tonight. It's as if all the world has come to a halt, and the only sound in the world is the thud of your heart, pounding in your chest.

Out in the darkness, Rusty begins to cry and asks if there's a villain in the house, like the bad guys always fighting Batman and Robin. Then he says, "What about Sam and the baby?" You can't believe you forgot about your other boys. Who will protect them? Searing pain zig zags through your chest. Rusty, waiting for your answer stares at you, only this time he notices the shotgun in your hand and starts to tremble. You drop the evil thing, push it away with your foot. You pull your son tight to your breast, wishing you could find words. Any words to make it all better. A few materialize before your eyes, but the letters are dancing and fly apart before you can speak one.

The voice of your neighbor reaches you before you see him cresting the hill between your lawns. He's running towards you, wrapping his robe tightly to his body.

The sight of him causes you to shatter inside, and that's when you crumble into the dew drenched grass.

Reaching out to him, you finally find your words and scream, "Help us! Help us! For the love of God, please help us!" into the black, silent night.

HAVE YOU EVER SEEN THE RAIN?

by James Burnham

"What does a blind man want with a shotgun?" the clerk asks.

"I don't see how that's any of your business?" I say, tapping my white cane against the cold, glass display. Lemon-lime nacho chipped bad breath, oiled metal, and day old socks waft in the air.

The crinkling of a tin can adds a dissonant overtone to the man's gurgling belch. "What you gonna shoot?"

"Anything I damn well please. You gonna sell me the thing or what?" I imagine his squishy face with French-fry pores lubricating double chins.

"No law against a blind man buying a gun. But you have to wait the ten-day cooling-off period first."

"Ten days? ´For what?"

He chuckles. "To keep you from shooting anything you damn well please."

"Well, that's absurd!"

"All the same," he says. "You have to wait ten days '´fore you can take one home. What are you looking for?"

"A pistol."

I hear heavy steps on tile floor moving away, keys jingling, something sliding, then the clop-clop of heavy boots returning.

"Try this one on for size. It's our newest nine millimeter."

I hold out my hands, palms up, to receive the steel, running my fingers along the muzzle until a picture forms in my mind's eye. It feels heavy for its size, sleek and cold. I find the trigger and turn the gun to measure its fit under my chin.

"Hey!" the man protests. "That's not funny."

I make like I meant to sniff the barrel. "Smells like gun powder. You sure it's new?"

"They fire them in the factory. Nothing more."

I turn it in my hands, satisfied. "I'll take it. Ten days you say?"

"Ten days."

I detest the idea of waiting, but there's nothing to be done about it. The thought that a man might change his mind in ten days baffles me. Ten days strengthen one's resolve. Ten days give time to make plans and calculate outcomes.

He takes my information. I sign a contract I cannot see and will return in ten days with cash enough for the balance and one box of ammunition. What a waste. One bullet is all I'll need.

My cane leads the way down the sidewalk. The air feels cold, but the sun is warm on my face between the trees. Crape Myrtle. I know from the scent of flowers mixing with fresh clover and something grassy, alfalfa perhaps. I sniffle and sneeze, then wipe my wet hand on my pants. I'll be up all night scratching itchy eyes.

Ten days.

I tap until the cane falls away from the curb and step off without hesitation. Twenty-three steps to the bus stop and a ten minute ride on the bus brings me to work.

"Hi, Larry!" Wendy calls from her desk. "Warm out there, huh?"

"I guess." My own desk sits against the back wall facing away from the windows. Our director figured a blind man wouldn't care which way he faces. Bastard.

"It's been slow. Just one call this morning from a talker. Nothing serious."

She's blinded by optimism and naïve enough to think she's actually making a difference. I know better. A seriously suicidal person cannot be saved by a stranger on the phone.

She bubbles on, "Do you want me to stay and keep you company?"

"I'll be fine."

"Call if things get busy."

"I will."

I wait until she departs and press the play button on the portable CD player sitting on my desk. The CD whirls to life and the sad musings of Mozart's *Requiem in D minor* fill the room.

When the phone rings, I stop the music.

"Meadowlands Suicide Hotline. How can I help?"

Choppy static answers.

"Meadowlands Suicide Hotline. If you don't talk, I can't help you."

Sniffling is followed by a young girl's thready voice. "Hello?"

"What's your name?"

"I don't want to say my name."

Fantastic. A slow goer. "You don't have to if you don't want to."

"I'm scared."

"Why?" The first rule is to keep them talking. "What are you afraid of?"

"Bella. My name is Bella."

Did she have to have that name? My words come slowly and deliberately. "Bella was my daughter's name, too."

Rule two: establish a rapport through common ground.

"You have a daughter?" she says.

I should hang up the phone right now, go home, and forget this place and its problems. But something in the girl's voice reminds of my duty. "Not anymore."

"Why not?"

"She died." Who's helping who here?

"I'm sorry." Her voice cracks. "I…have to go."

"Wait!" Take a deep breath. Focus. Keep her on the phone. "If I tell you about my Bella, will you tell me why you called?" A bargain. It's something.

"I don't want to talk about…"

"She was only eight years old…" I can hear her heavy breath over the line. She could hang up on me. Is it wrong that a part of me wants her to? "…when she died."

"I'm going to kill myself," she finally says.

There it is. Her cry for help. I check the Braille clock and make notes on the call sheet. Now for the most important question. "How do you plan to kill yourself?"

"I don't know."

A pretender. I should hang up on her and save us both the trouble of a drawn out conversation that goes nowhere. But it's better to keep her on the line for the log. The longer they talk, the better our funding. "Do you want to talk about it?"

"I have pills and a razor blade, but…"

She does have a plan. Two plans. Those serious about committing suicide have a course of action. They stand on the edge of a cliff leaning, hoping to fall. The primary question is why hasn't she already jumped? Does she want to be saved, or is she simply seeking an audience?

"You're not alone, Bella. I'm with you."

"No one cares about me," she whispers. "I have to go…"

"Wait! Where are you now?"

She sniffles and sucks in a long breath. "Why?"

"Because I want to know."

"In the closet. I sound pretty messed up, huh?"

"We're all messed up, Bella. Living is trying to find that one thing that keeps us going. My daughter was that to me."

"And now she's gone."

Perceptive. "She's not gone to me."

Her voice turns frantic. "I really have to go. Bill's home!"

"Bella? Can we talk again?"

"Maybe."

"I'll wait if you promise to call. Will you call me back tonight?"

"I'll try."

"I need you to promise me."

"Fine. I promise."

I hang up the phone and finish my notes.

There are no other calls that afternoon or evening, what we refer to as primetime, which has nothing to do with the frequency of calls and everything to do with television programming. Otherwise, primetime would be from one to three in the morning. We call that the graveyard shift because that's when most suicides occur.

She has not called when my relief arrives at midnight. I should have guessed. Kids bluff more than adults.

I take the bus home and turn on the television for company, take a Benadryl, and relax in my recliner. Bella's picture finds its way into my left hand and a bottle of bourbon into my right. I fall asleep remembering how beautiful she looked that morning in her white dress and yellow ribbons.

I wake to puffy, burning eyes. Another day. Another long wait for sleep. The eye drops sting, falling cold from the sterile bottle, but they help revive me. I brew coffee and pour the thick juice into my thermos, add a few splashes of bourbon, then head to work.

"What gives, Larry?" Wendy asks as I place my lunch bag on my desk. "You're three hours early."

"Bored. It's too quiet at home. Any calls last night? A teen girl, perhaps?"

"One call this morning, but it was an older gentleman. Why?"

"Hoping for a call back. I'm gonna sit here and listen to my music for a while. You can go on home, if you want. I'll clock you out."

"Are you sure?"

"Positive."

"Thanks, Larry. You're the best."

It's not until midnight that the phone rings again.

"Hello?"

"Hi," she says. "I was hoping you would answer."

"Bella. I knew you'd keep your promise."

"I couldn't call last night. Things got really bad here."

"Are you in danger now?"

She sighs. "It doesn't matter anymore. I'm leaving for good soon."

Her meaning is clear to me. "That again? You're too young to want to die."

She doesn't speak, and I hate the silence. I hate waiting alone in the darkness for someone else's voice.

She says, "You promised to tell me about Bella."

My sweet Bella. I've spoken to no one about her since the funeral. "She was beautiful," I begin. "She had a laugh like summer rain and eyes as blue as the sky. She loved to jump on my back. I'd put her on my shoulders and carry her anywhere she wanted."

"You sound like a good father. She was lucky."

"I tried." My throat feels dry, my eyes scratchy. I should have taken another Benadryl.

"I hate my dad," she says.

"You don't mean that."

"I do. I hate him."

"Why?"

She pauses. "How did Bella die?"

I find a pencil with my finger and roll it back and forth on the desk. "We were at the park," I say. "I'd bought her a red kite with a long blue tail for her birthday. How hard is it to fly a kite? All you do is hold a string and the wind does all the work, right? It was foolish to think that a blind man could teach his daughter how to fly a kite. I couldn't see where it fell when the wind died or see her running after it into the street. She never saw the car coming."

"God. I'm sorry." Her voice fades away, then returns barely audible. "Can you keep a secret?"

The pencil freezes under my finger. "Of course. Unless you're in danger. Then, I have to call someone."

"You have to promise me you won't tell anyone."

They tell us not to make promises, but I've lost too many callers playing by the rules. "I promise I won't say anything unless you tell me to."

"Bill's not my real dad. They aren't even married. But, he makes me call him daddy. He says he loves me. And, he's always staring at me. He touches me when Mom's not looking."

A part of me hopes that I misunderstood her. "Does he hurt you?"

"It hurt a lot the first time."

The first time? How many times? I lay my forehead against the palm of my hand, my elbow resting on the desk. Primal anger only a father could know begins to burn within my belly. "How old are you?"

"Thirteen."

"Does your mother know?"

"Sometimes, I think she does. She looks at me with angry eyes."

"I mean, does she know that he rapes you?" The words feel ugly on my tongue. Foul. Dirty. But I need clarification to be sure that I didn't misunderstand her.

She begins to sob. "I don't know."

"You have to tell her, Bella."

"I can't."

"You have to. It's not your fault."

She's crying loudly now. "That's why I called you."

"I'm just a voice on the phone. I'm not real."

"You're real to me. You can help. You're the reason I called back."

"The only way I can help is by calling the police. They'll arrest him and protect you."

"No!" she protests, pleading. "You promised me."

"Bella…"

"He'll hurt us. You don't know him."

"I have to…"

The line goes dead. I slam the phone down in frustration. I've lost her. She reached out to me for help, and I let her down.

I sit alone in my recliner playing the conversation over and over in my mind and thinking about what I could have done differently. Each agonizing second, each click of the hand on the clock, fills me with guilt. Thus, the night stretches on forever…and the next day…and the next night.

I go into work early on the fifth day to find she still hasn't called. When the night monitor arrives, I send her away. She protests, but I cut her off. I tell her I lost a caller, that I have to be the one to answer the phone. In the end, she understands.

Loneliness embraces me in the darkness. Still, no call.

Six days. Seven.

On the eighth day, I dream of red kites and screeching tires. A faceless girl calls to me from the shadows. I search but cannot find her and wake to sweaty sheets clinging to my back.

Eight.

I ready myself by taking care of the small details so no one else will have to. I write a thank you letter to my neighbor for her annual holiday bread and another to my wife's sister. We never got along all that great, but she was there when Mary had cancer and again when Bella died. I struggle most with the last letter—the explanation. It's remarkably short for all that I want to say.

Nine.

I stop by the florist on the way to work to buy a spring arrangement for the office. It smells of roses and lilac. The lady calls her son to carry them for me, and I tip him twenty dollars for his trouble.

Wendy beams. "They're beautiful! What are they for?"

"No reason." I wonder what she will think when I'm gone. Will she blame herself for not recognizing the signs?

I eat my sandwich and settle in to wait.

When Bella finally calls, she sounds frantic, her voice pitched high. "Are you there?"

"It's me."

"Thank God. I need your help."

"What happened?"

"Can you come and get me? Please?"

Every bit of training and common sense warns me to say no, but I can't. Something about this girl has crawled under my skin and taken hold. We talk to callers, help them feel better, then direct them to professionals. But are we really helping them? Who knows? Perhaps my last act on this earth could be to make a real difference for this one girl, this Bella.

"Where are you?"

"I don't know. I ran away this morning and rode the bus all day long. The driver told me I had to get off. Please, come and get me. I'm scared."

"Do you recognize anything? What's around you?"

"I don't know."

"Look around. Listen. Tell me everything you see and hear."

"There's a park and a church across the street."

It couldn't be. Irony in her deepest winter would never be so cruel. "Is there a fountain across the street from the church?"

"It's too dark to see."

"Close your eyes and listen. Tell me if you hear two different sounds, one sharp like water spraying from a hose, and another bubbling sound, like a bath tub being filled."

"I think so."

"I know where you are. Go to the fountain and wait by the benches under the gas lamps. I'll be there as quickly as I can."

"Hurry. I'm scared."

"I'm on my way."

I abandon the suicide hotline and hail a cab.

"West Church Street and Clay, please. As quickly as you can."

"You got it."

I listen to the sound of tires on asphalt as we drive and the clickety-click of the bridge as we cross the river near the park. I pay the fare and step out onto the curb. The cool air blowing across fresh cut grass triggers memories of other visits filled with wild-flower bouquets, warm picnic blankets, and laughter. These are the precious memories that I've tried so hard to forget.

"Bella?" I call out. No answer. I keep tapping and walking and calling out.

"Is it you?" her voice says timidly from my right.

"It's me." I turn and tap closer.

"You're blind?"

"I'm Larry."

Her arms wrap around my waist and squeeze hard. I can feel her body trembling as she weeps. With her head just reaching my chest, I envelope her petite form in a cautious embrace, my cheek resting on strawberry scented hair.

After several minutes of swaying in the breeze, she pulls away. "How did you find me so fast?"

"I know this park well. I used to come here with my Bella."

"Oh," she says, and adds cautiously, "the kite?"

"Yes. This was our park." I don't tell her that this is also the church where I married my wife, buried her, then buried our child, that I haven't been here since I told the pastor goodbye. "Do you like pizza?"

"Yes." She continues to grip my arm as if she might lose me.

"There's a great place not a block from here. Let's have a slice."

She hooks her arm in mine and guides me as I lead her through the park and down the street. I can smell the yeast dough even before we round the corner.

"Larry!" Vincinzo greets us, his Sicilian accent as strong as ever. "It's been years. How are you, old buddy?"

"Fine," I say.

"The usual? Pepperoni and pineapple, wasn't it?"

I lean to my left and whisper. "How does that sound?"

"Okay," she says.

"That'll be great," I say to Vincinzo.

We sit in a booth next to an old jukebox that still plays forty-fives. Classic Americana fills her belly. Elvis. Beach Boys. Select country. Even the Rat Pack.

Vinnie brings us sodas. Bella makes bubbles with her straw.

"I really wasn't that scared," she says. "I've run away before. I hid in the school gym last time and slept on the mats and took showers in the locker room."

"You sounded scared on the phone," I say.

"Mom thinks I should be an actress. When I'm old enough, I'm moving to Hollywood to be a movie star. Maybe a singer. I can play the guitar pretty good. My granddaddy taught me when I was little." She blows more bubbles. "Do you have any quarters?"

"Sure." I fish out a couple coins from my pocket and offer them in my palm.

I hear a quarter fall through the machine. Mechanics whir to life and a record drops onto the turntable. Creedence Clearwater Revival's smoky tenor fills the restaurant. Mary's favorite song.

Have you ever seen the rain?

I have. I'm still drowning in it.

Bella slides across the booth opposite me, humming the song in perfect pitch. I hear crayons moving across paper. I've hung similar pictures on the refrigerator many times before.

She says in a happy singsong voice, "Do you want to have sex with me?"

My mind reels. I nearly drop my glass. "Why would you ask me that?"

"I don't mind if you want to. I've had sex before." She touches my hand. "And you're nice."

I snap my hand back as if it had been burned. "You shouldn't say that."

"You are, though."

"It doesn't matter. You shouldn't even think such things."

I wish I could see her face and know her thoughts. I wonder if she's looking at mine. Does she see the disgust I feel?

"Are you mad at me?" she asks.

I shake my head. "No, sweetheart. Not with you. With those who did this to you."

"You mean Daddy?"

"Don't call him that."

She giggles. "He likes it. He has me call him all sorts of things when Mommy's not around."

"How old were you when he first…?"

"Had sex?" The giggling subsides. "Eleven. It was my birthday. He said he had a special present for me. You're not going to make me go home, are you? I'm never going back there again."

"I won't make you do anything you don't want to."

"And you won't let him hurt me anymore?"

"No, Bella. He won't."

"Promise?"

"I promise."

She makes bubbles in her glass again and continues humming along with the music. The pizza is delivered and she speaks between bites about her grandfather who rode horses and once drove a submarine.

I feel something pushing against my hand and take the paper and feel the crayon with my fingertips. "What's this?"

"I drew you a picture. It's the park, and your daughter is flying her kite. I wish you could see it."

Half of me wants to crumple it up and toss it in the pizza oven. The other half trembles with thankfulness. "Come on," I say.

"Where are we going?"

"Home."

"Your home?"

"Yes."

I consider my decision during the cab ride back to my apartment. I should take her straight to the police. She's been abused and they would take care of her, give her to a foster family, arrest the boyfriend and her mother. But what good would that do? I've received calls from foster kids, too. More often than not, their new family is worse than the old one.

I unlock the door and push it open. The couch squeaks under her weight. Then, I hear her heels land one at a time on the coffee table.

"Please, don't." I say.

"Sorry." They fall to the floor.

I place my cane in its usual place and take a seat next to her. "Are you tired?"

"Yes, but not sleepy."

"Would you like to watch television?"

"Okay." She finds the remote herself and flips through the channels, settling on a popular sit-com. "Larry?"

"Yes?"

"I'm sorry about what I said before. I really didn't mean it."

"It's okay."

"Sometimes I say things I don't mean. I don't know why."

"It's not your fault. You're just a child."

"I'm a woman."

"No. Having sex with a man doesn't make you a woman."

I hear the same sad tone in her voice that I heard on the phone. "He ruined me, didn't he?"

"No, Bella. No one can ruin another person."

"But, he did." She sniffles as laughter from the television fills the room. Several minutes pass before she speaks again. "Have you always been blind?"

"No. I'm diabetic. That means my body can't control the sugar in my blood. Sometimes people like me go blind."

"How old were you when it happened?"

"Thirty-five."

"I'm sorry. Kind of makes my life seem not so bad."

How could anyone have a worse life? I can't imagine what a thirteen-year-old goes through wondering each night if he will come again.

She yawns and blinks twice. "I guess I'm sleepier than I thought."

"I'll get you a pillow and a blanket."

Returning with the items from the linen closet, I find her already deeply asleep. I gently lift her head and place the pillow underneath it, wondering what color her hair is. Maybe soft amber, like my Bella's? I sit in my chair with the bottle of bourbon in hand and listen to her deep, even breaths flow in and out. But I can't drink. Getting drunk feels inappropriate tonight.

When I wake, I find her at the kitchen table crunching through a bowl of cereal.

"Good morning," she chimes. "I hope you don't mind."

What was I thinking bringing an abused child into my house? I choose my words carefully. "You need to call your mother and let her know that you're safe. They're probably worried sick about you."

"Doubt it. They don't care what I do. Sometimes, I don't see them for two or three days straight."

"All the same. I'd like you to try." I hear her spoon fall against the edge of the bowl.

"But, you promised."

"I know. And I'm not making you. I'm asking you."

"Fine," she says after a long moment. "But, you won't make me go if I don't want to?"

"Not until you're ready."

I direct her to the phone and settle into a chair to wait.

"Mom? Yes, it's me. Stop crying. I had to get away for a while. What's wrong?" Her throat sounds tight, her words strangled and tinged with fear. "I can't understand what you're saying. Stay there, okay? I'm coming straight home."

The air rushes around me as she moves.

"I have to go!"

I rise and follow her into the living room. "What happened?"

"She's high as a kite. Can you..."

"I'll take you home."

"Thanks, Larry." The room is suddenly quiet. "I wish you could be my daddy."

It takes fifteen minutes for the cab to arrive. I make a mental note of the address and pay attention to the sounds as we drive. I'm not familiar with this part of town, so tracking the turns and judging distance is difficult. When we slow, Bella springs from the cab even before it has come to a complete stop.

"What is this place?" I ask the driver and hand over the fare. "And, where did she go?"

"Hillside Apartments. She's entering the first building on the left. Downstairs."

"Can you wait for me?"

"Only a few minutes."

"Give me five, please."

I take my cane and follow after her the best I can, but the unknown terrain is unsettling. Each tap, each step, is an uncertain leap of faith. Just when I think I have lost my direction, I hear Bella's voice echoing through the hallway.

"Mom? Please, wake up!"

I pause at the threshold. The apartment reeks of drugs and booze and vomit and rotten trash, and I know it's just a matter of time before Bella runs away again. She'll never find a normal life in this place.

"Bella?'

A faint, disoriented voice answers, "Bee? Is that you?"

"What did you take this time? Tell me!"

"Nothing. Baby. I swear."

"You're lying again. Why do you cover for him when he beats you like this?"

"He didn't."

"But your face is swollen black and blue!"

"I fell, sweetheart. Billy didn't do anything. I swear."

I step inside the apartment and feel crunching under my feet. Kneeling, my hand finds a broken plastic container and capsules scattered about it. I gather them up and slip them into my pocket.

"I hate you!" Bella suddenly cries out. "I hate you! I hate you! I hate you!" I hear a loud slap and her mother cry out.

"Bella?" I say, trying to think of some way to help.

"Leave me alone!" she screams. "All of you!"

I hear the front door slam shut behind me.

"Who the hell are you?" her mother yells. "Get outa my house!"

You don't deserve her, I want to say, but retreat into the hallway and listen for any sign of Bella. Children play nearby. The smell of marijuana wafts from somewhere upstairs. But there is no sign of her. I ask the taxi driver if he had seen her come out. He hadn't.

Another sleepless night.

Ten.

"There he is," the foul-smelling merchant says when I enter his gun shop. "Has it been ten days already?"

"Finally," I say.

"She's worth the wait. I cleaned her up for you real good. Only one box of bullets, huh?"

"Just one."

He takes the bills and hands me change. I sign more papers and wait, gun in hand.

"Are we done?" I ask.

"Easy as that. Be careful out there. Big storm on the way."

He has no idea.

The rain begins as soon as I step out of the gun shop. The air smells electric and the gusting wind feels icy cold. I shiver and hurry to the bus stop. Once home, I dump the bullets onto the kitchen table. Some fall to the floor. The sound reminds me of popcorn kernels bouncing off a hard pan. I find them one by one, slip them into the clip, and slide the clip into the gun.

It's time.

I haven't used the record player since Mary died. She loved the old scratchy sound of needle on wax and would spend the entire afternoon visiting pawn shops in search of her melodic ambrosia. We laughed for so long the first time she used those words.

Someone told me long ago…There's a calm before the storm…

The ice cubes clink as they fall into the glass and crack as the bourbon drowns them. Bittersweet and sharp tastes the amber liquid on my tongue.

I know…It's been comin' for some time…

I take a glass, the bottle, and the gun with me to the couch. Something crinkles under me. Bella's picture. It smells of crayon. The paper, brittle. I begin to crumple it up, but decide otherwise. Carefully, I fold it in half and half again and stuff it into my shirt pocket.

When it's over so they say…It'll rain a sunny day…I know…Shining down like water…

A gust of wind rattles the windows and whistles under the front door. I pick up the gun and place the barrel in my mouth. The metal tastes like oil and cold blood.

I want to know…have you ever seen the rain…

How hard will I have to pull the trigger? Will my life flash before my eyes? I think about Mary and her infectious smile. I hear her giggling under the sheets and singing in the park. The park. Bella. She came home from the hospital Sunday morning. God how she hated peas and slimy peaches and loved sugar cookies. I remember her first day of preschool and how we cried, all three of us.

Slowly, I squeeze the trigger.

The phone rings for the first time in six months. Damn! I should let it go.

"Hello?"

"Larry! He's gonna kill us!"

"Bella?"

"He said I took his pills. I swear I didn't!"

Feeling inside my pocket, I remember the capsules. I took them!

"You have to help us. I believe him this time, Larry. I do!"

I measure the gun's weight. Maybe there's a way I can help her after all? "Okay," I say with determination. "I'm on my way."

"Hurry!"

The taxi takes twice as long as it should to arrive. He says a tree fell onto a power line, and none of the street lights are working.

"Hillside Apartments," I say, not caring about his excuses. The gun feels cold in my hand, my hand warm in my coat pocket.

I hear the clap of thunder and deep rumbling nearby. The gusting wind causes the car to swerve side to side. Each tire hydroplanes on its own accord and produces spitting sounds when the water gives way to the rubber. The driver curses and slows down. I encourage him to hurry.

"Sure you want to be out in this?" the driver says as I open the door.

"Keep the change," I say.

"Damn straight!"

I lean forward into the wind and push my way up the sidewalk and into the shelter of the hallway. The door to Bella's apartment is already open. "Hello?" I call.

No answer. I step through, listening, and hear whimpering coming from somewhere inside. I follow the sound, using my cane to find the way. "Bella?" I call out again.

Gurgling rises from my left. "Help me," someone pleads. Her mother?

"Where's Bella?" I ask.

She tries to speak again but can only produce a wet cough. I kneel beside her and reach out. Her hands feels sticky. I find a knife in her belly.

"Bella!" I cry out.

"Who the hell are you?"

Strong hands grab me by the collar. I grab hold of the knife and feel it slide out as a man yanks me up and spins me around. I think to lash out, but his fist slams into my cheek before I can react. The knife clatters to the floor. My head strikes the wall, and I slump down next to Bella's mother.

He grabs me by the collar again, this time the front, and leans so close I can feel his breath on my cheeks and spit on my lips. He reeks of alcohol and sweat. "What are you doing here, man?" His grip loosens a little. "What's wrong with you? You blind or something?"

I hear Bella's voice nearby. "Leave him alone, Bill! I swear, I'll…"

"Shut your face!"

Bella gasps and cries out, "Mommy? Is she…?"

He lets go of me and moves away. "Put that knife down, little girl. Or, you'll find the sharp end yourself."

"I hate you!"

I hear a burst of movement, followed by a dull thud.

He swears. "Try and stab me, you little bitch? Now I'm gonna stick you!"

"Let go! Get off me!" she screams.

The sound of his zipper is unmistakable. His fist lands another loud blow, and she begins to cry.

"No. No. Please!" She pleads. "Larry!"

I hear cloth ripping over his maniacal laughter. "Open your legs!"

The gun finds its way into my hands as Bella shrieks and he exhales. I use his breathless grunts of sick satisfaction for aim. My ears ring from the concussive report.

"What the hell?" He laughs. "A blind man with a gun?"

I squeeze again and again until the clip is empty and the room quiet.

I crawl towards them and slip on blood. Bella finds my arms and sobs. I pull her as close as I can and tell her that everything's going to be okay.

It's not until her body goes limp that I realize something is wrong.

"Bella?"

"I don't feel anything," she says with a voice eerily similar to her mother's.

"No! Bella. Please…"

"I knew you'd come," she says.

My mind races, but I can't move. I should call for help. I should leave her and find a phone.

"Freeze!"

I let go of Bella as rough hands grab me and push me to the floor. Sharp cuffs cut into my wrists.

"You have the right to remain silent…" the voice begins.

When finished, another officer says, "Looks like they both had their way with her. Shot the man and stabbed the woman with this knife here. She probably walked in on them…"

My body feels numb. I can't speak.

"Get him out of here," the second officer says.

I'm propelled through the rain and into a squad car where they make me wait until I'm shivering from the cold. When an officer arrives, he whistles from high to low and tells me not to expect any special treatment because I'm blind.

The room in the police station is even colder than the squad car. I tremble for an hour before the door opens and someone enters.

"You can take off the cuffs," the voice says.

A key is inserted and the cuffs fall away. I rub my wrists and push wet hair out of my face. The tears remain.

"No one's going to make a stink about a dead drug dealer," the voice said. "But, why did you kill the woman and then shoot that girl?"

"Is she…?" I can't finish the sentence.

"Don't know yet. Still in surgery."

I drop my forehead into my hands and press my palms into my eyes. I should have pulled the trigger when I had a chance. Now…I clear my throat. "Can I have a glass of water, please?"

"There's a bottle in front of you. Your neighbor says she saw the girl at your place. What was she doing there?"

I take a drink and crinkle the plastic in my hands.

"Did she bring you drugs?"

"She needed my help," I say. My voice sounds strange, distant in my own ears.

"I see. Is that why she drew this? Did you buy her this kite?"

My hand reaches for the picture in my shirt pocket, but the pocket is empty. I don't even remember them taking it.

"Is this where you met? In this park?"

"It's not what you think," I try to say, but the words catch in my throat. I can't breathe. What have I done? Please, God, let her be okay! My hands fall to my side. The pills! Had they taken them as well?

"We'll sit here as long as it takes for you to start talking. How long have you known the girl? Did you have your way with her first?"

Dear, God. Please, have mercy on my soul. I cram the pills into my mouth and swiftly gulp a drink of water.

"Hey!"

Hands grab me and pull at my jaw. I bite down hard on probing fingers. Someone curses and strikes me across the temple.

I fall dizzy to the floor with the taste of cotton candy on my tongue and the smell of caramel in my nose.

"Get a doctor!"

My heart pounds in my ears. Images and sounds flash through my mind. I hear my grandmother's voice and the birds in her garden, the smell of fresh rolls. She baked those on Sundays. And Mary. My sweet, sweet Mary. I remember our first kiss and her soft breast against my arm as we walked. I remember the picnic at the end of the runway with the most beautiful sunset. I taste red wine on her lips. "Yes," she said, breathless, and we made love under the stars.

And Bella. My beautiful Bella. I remember her first steps and her first words, butterfly kisses, and up-reaching arms.

I'm aware of everything and nothing. I remember everything and nothing. So, this is what death feels like, everything and nothing? My body tingles and feels numb, and I wonder how that can be. I'm overwhelmed and disappointed...scared of what will happen next.

I hear the sound of gunshots and envision Bella lying bleeding in my arms. Did I kill her? I should feel guilty, but I don't. Either way, she's free.

Mary sits next to me warming by the fire. "She looks like you," she says, her words filled with love.

I take my Bella and kiss her gently on the forehead. "She's the most beautiful thing I've never seen."

ONE STANDARD DEVIATION

by Diane Byington

I was old but not deaf. I easily discerned the familiar jibes as I made my way through the restaurant. "That's Congresswoman Underhill. Boy, is she over the hill." "Yeah, and she'll be under it pretty soon." I didn't respond, partly because I was late for my party. Also, I didn't want to embarrass the speakers, who might once have been my constituents. I loved that they still recognized me. I even agreed with the sentiment, which was truer than they realized.

My family--two daughters, sons-in-law, and three grandchildren--had gathered at my favorite Italian restaurant to celebrate my birthday. They stood and clapped when I swept into the room. I smiled, pleased that I could still make an entrance. "Hello, everybody. Thanks for coming." I glanced at a stack of presents and a cake with so many candles that the entire room might combust when lit. Time for that later.

Most of my family members had traveled a long distance for this occasion, and I hadn't seen many of them for a while. We hugged and posed for a family photo. The room felt alive with conversation and caring as everyone enjoyed mounds of Italian food. However, I was too nervous about my announcement to do more than nibble a few bites of veal parmigiana.

I took a deep breath and rapped on my water glass. I cleared my throat and said, "I'm surprised the cake wasn't too heavy for you to carry." Small laugh. They probably thought the same thing. I smiled and continued. "You can light the candles in a few minutes. For now, I have something to tell you." I paused, waiting for the suspense to build. Finally, I said, "Tomorrow, as you know, is my eighty-eighth birthday. And I'm choosing to go on the Ice."

My grandchildren dropped their forks and stared at me in horror. "No…" said Karen, my oldest daughter, her voice just shy of a shriek. "I won't let you."

I appreciated her concern, even though I wondered about its sincerity. Karen only managed to break away from her high-powered job for a few days to visit every year on my birthday. I told myself not to be cynical about her reaction, today of all days.

Gail, my youngest daughter, shook her head in dismay but didn't argue. She lived just across town and dutifully visited me every

Sunday afternoon. She knew better than to try to change my mind. Good girl.

Eventually, Karen calmed down and allowed me to proceed. "I realize this is an unpopular decision. But, it's irrevocable. I've already registered, and I'm leaving in the morning. I hope you can support my choice, even if you don't agree with it."

"Why would you do such a crazy thing?" asked Karen, her voice trembling. "Especially without consulting us first. You voted against the IceFloe."

"Yes, that's true. If you remember, my side lost. The IceFloe is now the law of the land."

"No, it isn't. It's optional," said Will, Karen's husband.

I sighed. "Optional, yes, but only if you have enough money to pay for medical care." I held up my hand. "I know I could do it. But it isn't right for the wealthy to avoid the fate of the poor. Tomorrow I will join my sisters and brothers on the Ice."

Ten years before, when huge numbers of elderly people, pregnant women, and babies began falling ill from a mutated version of the Zika virus, health care resources strained near the breaking point. The newly elected President came up with the IceFloe concept as a way to deal with people who were one standard deviation above the average age of death. For women, eighty-eight became the magic number. For men, it was eighty-five. The President explained to the country that the IceFloe followed the actions of the Inuit, who placed their elders on icebergs to travel to their deaths. In this case, there wouldn't be an actual iceberg--just a walled off area to which the eldest among us would be sent to die on their own, without exploiting government resources.

I organized the opposition in Congress. However, Zika was running rampant through the population, and people were terrified. The plan to build the IceFloe progressed. I resigned after I lost the vote, ostensibly to take care of my husband as he battled Zika. He died a few weeks later, and I didn't have the heart to run for office again. I'd needed time to grieve, both for Paul and for my beloved country that had taken such a wrong turn.

Now, I struggled to summon enough breath to blow out all those candles. I opened my gifts and thanked the givers, who continued to argue with me. The waiters ended up throwing away most of the cake because my family had lost their appetite. Eventually, I grew too tired to squabble anymore. I had to leave before anyone guessed my secret. I thanked them all for coming and hugged each one goodbye.

I had prepared a little speech for this moment and delivered it flawlessly. I told them not to mourn for me. I had had a full life, I missed Paul and would be joining him before long, and I loved them all. True enough. But, in actuality, I expected to be back home in a few weeks. I hoped they wouldn't be even angrier when they found out that my heartfelt speech had been premature.

Chloe, my youngest granddaughter, drove me home. In the car, she said, "Grandma, are you sure about this?"

I nodded. "Oh, yes, I'm sure. This story is going to blow the cover off the myth that old people are happy on the Ice. The law will be repealed when people hear about the terrible conditions inside."

"And I'm the only one you've told about what you're doing?"

"Good lord, girl. We've talked this whole thing to death. You know you're the only one. Your mom and aunt couldn't keep a secret if their lives depended on it."

"All right, then." She parked the car, and we went inside my condo. I closed the drapes while Chloe brought out the communication device designed by her sympathetic FBI contact. He had embedded it into a silver flag pin. I loved flags and would be proud to wear such a beautiful symbol of my patriotism. One of the diamonds on the pin, when pressed, provided a direct link to Chloe.

I cupped the pin in my hands. Strangely, it felt warm to my touch. "I can call you on this, right?" I asked. "But you can't call me?"

Chloe sighed. "You know that's right," she said in a tight voice. "It's what you insisted on."

"I don't want to get in trouble if you call at an inopportune moment. I don't know what I'll face when I get there, so I need to choose the time when we talk." I'd explained this a dozen times before.

She shrugged. "All right, Grandma. I don't agree, but I set it up the way you wanted." She paused. "Listen, we weren't able to test this, for obvious reasons. My FBI contact thinks it will work, but he isn't sure."

I nodded. "That's fine, honey. All you can do is your best."

Chloe frowned. "Mom will never forgive me for helping you if you end up dying out there. Having you around is more important than any story." Tears welled up in her eyes. "Grandma, I know we've talked and talked about this, but now that it's happening, I'm not sure it's the right thing to do."

I shook my head and squared my shoulders, which weren't as sturdy as they had once been. I tried to keep my voice from trembling as I said, "It's my decision, not yours, and I've made it. I'll do it alone if I have to." Chloe worked as an investigative reporter for a major newspaper, one of the few left in a changed world. She would write the story well and maybe even win a Pulitzer. I hadn't undertaken this project solely to help her, but breaking the story would probably assure her career.

I dug two sealed envelopes out of my purse. "Here," I said, my tone softening. "Give these letters to your mother and aunt if it doesn't work out. They explain what I'm trying to do. I take all the responsibility. Sweetie, even if I die in there, it'll be okay. I'm old, and I'm going to die soon anyway. This way I have a chance of making a difference."

"I don't agree. You've got lots of good years left. You can always do this later." We stared at each other for a long moment. I kept my eyes steady on hers, even though part of me agreed with Chloe and wanted to give up on my crazy plan. But, I owed it to the future to try to fix the country's terrible mistake.

Eventually, Chloe said, "Oh, all right. But shouldn't we figure out a failsafe method to get you out of there if this doesn't work? Like storming the gate in two weeks or something?"

We had talked that one to death, too. "No," I said. "I'll let you know what I find. I'll call you tomorrow evening after I get there, and we'll decide how to proceed." I squeezed my granddaughter's hands. "This is going to work. And, if by some chance it doesn't, then go on with your life. Remember me as I am now, not as I'll become later."

We hugged. I held Chloe as tightly as my weakened arms would allow. I hadn't told my family, not even Chloe, about the congestive heart failure that sucked my energy and would soon end my life. I hoped I would have time to complete this one last thing before I died.

After Chloe left, I packed a small bag with a few clothes and fell into bed, exhausted. I thought through the arrangements. Will agreed to take me to the train station in the morning. I'd chosen him because he would not make a scene. I hated to leave my home and family, but I would be leaving them soon, one way or another.

The next morning I swallowed a handful of medications with two cups of coffee, turned off the coffee maker and washed my cup for the last time, then dried it carefully and placed it in the cupboard. I left the pill bottles on the counter.

Instead of Will, my whole family arrived at 9 a.m. "What is this?" I asked.

Karen stepped forward. "We don't agree with what you're doing, but we won't let you go on this journey alone."

I hugged my daughters and tried not to cry. If I started, I might never quit, and I wanted my family to remember me as the strong woman they had always known.

The special train stopped at our town once a day, at 10 a.m., and this day it chugged into the station right on schedule. Everyone hugged me one last time, and Will helped me up the stairs. I paused to wave goodbye. Karen gave me a copy of the family photograph from the night before, and Gail handed me a lunch bag with a chicken salad sandwich, as though I were heading off to school. We laughed, and it broke the tension a little.

"We'll be thinking of you," Gail said, "and always wishing you had trusted us to take care of you at the end. It's breaking our hearts, you know." She shook her head. "You always were too stubborn for your own good."

I nodded and found my seat. Even though it was only mid-morning, I accepted a glass of wine from the porter and kept a smile set on my face. At last, the train started moving. I watched the people I loved grow smaller and smaller, and reminded myself that this wasn't really my last goodbye. But it felt so very, very real.

I allowed myself to cry then, for a long time. This felt like the most ridiculous thing I'd ever done, even more foolish than running for Congress the first time. I could have stayed home and been a full-time wife and mother, and even had a regular job if I'd wanted one. Instead, I'd shuffled back and forth to Washington for years, allowing Paul to raise the girls and take care of the house. Now, my daughters were near-strangers, dutiful, but emotionally distant from me. Even worse, every good thing I'd done in Congress had been overturned by the last administration.

Eventually, my tears wore themselves out. Feeling sorry for myself was a waste of time. I'd never really considered whether I'd wanted to do those things I just did. No, I'd felt compelled to run for Congress, to try to make the country a better place. And, here I was—again--trying to rescue the country from itself.

I looked around and counted six women and two men traveling with me. Three of them were on oxygen, which would probably be removed at the gate, and two used walkers. I assumed they would be allowed to keep the walkers, although I didn't know for sure. What happened on the IceFloe was a closely held secret. None of us knew what we would encounter, and fear was etched onto everyone's faces. One woman asked over and over where we were going. Nobody answered.

I seemed to be the healthiest of the group, even with my heart problem. That didn't surprise me. Most people who went on the Ice were poor, and their health was generally worse than the middle-class or wealthy. I reminded myself that everyone dies. Maybe the Ice was more humane than being warehoused in nursing homes or hooked up to all kinds of equipment in a hospital. The opposition spouted this argument all the time and, until today, I had considered it pure propaganda. I'd argued for increased hospice care, humane and relatively inexpensive, or expanded home health care. Not the Ice. That was too extreme. But nobody had listened to me.

I drank my wine and watched the miles fly by. The train stopped at every town along the way, and one or two old people got on. Some left crying families behind, but most were alone. I considered what little I knew about our destination.

An IceFloe existed in every state, funded by a mixture of federal and state monies. In my state, ten-foot high walls surrounded what had originally been three square miles of majestic trees and wildflower-covered hills. Only residents were allowed inside. Since they couldn't leave or communicate with the outside world, details about the IceFloe remained elusive.

I'd read that residents were housed in apartment buildings, with meals prepared in communal kitchens. A small health clinic provided minimal care. No outside medical staff was allowed, no real medical supplies provided. The residents were expected to live out what time they had left with minimal support, then die quickly and naturally. "Like it would have been on the iceberg," the new President had said when he signed the bill into law. Then, he'd pasted that fake smile on his face, and I had thought I would gag.

I'd hoped that public opinion might be shifting as young people lost grandparents to the Ice. My first-hand account of abysmal conditions inside might help repeal this terrible law.

In mid-afternoon, I made out a tall wall in the distance that looked like it might surround a castle. Of course, there was no castle, no moat, and no way out once you passed inside. As we came closer, I saw electronic boxes affixed to the wall every six feet or so. They must be the jamming devices. I'd never understood why the law prohibited residents from communicating with the outside world. They were part of the package, though. Residents were on an IceFloe traveling away from civilization, never to be heard from again.

The train slowed, then stopped. Porters helped us down the steps and handed us our luggage. Our small group, huddled together, walked into an air-conditioned vestibule. Smiling young people asked us to sign releases saying we entered the IceFloe of our own free will, without coercion. Our bags were checked and contraband—mostly medications and cell phones—confiscated. Eventually, we were ushered into the main reception building. I patted the pin on my blouse. The guards hadn't discovered it, so I was in the clear. Relief flooded over me with such intensity that I feared I might faint. But, I stayed upright and tried to appear nonchalant about going to my death.

Without our handlers, we shuffled through the entry doors and onto the Ice. I looked around, wishing I had brought a camcorder to document my journey. It wouldn't have been allowed, of course. I'd known there wouldn't be any ice, but I'd expected to see frail elders writhing in pain, like in one of Dante's circles of hell, or skeletal people dying on the grounds. Truthfully, I'd expected something reminiscent of Auschwitz. Without medication or health care providers, how could conditions be anything other than horrible?

Instead, I walked into a sunlit garden overflowing with blooming flowers and ripe vegetables. Women clothed in bright dresses moved around the raised beds as they harvested, weeded, and chatted with each other. They waved at us but continued their work. I looked around in wonder. This seemed more like a park than a prison.

Two women holding clipboards met our group. They checked off names from the list provided by a customs agent and directed each arrival to an apartment. The woman who met me read my name and looked up. “Lucy Underhill. My, my. I never thought I’d see you here.” She smiled and reached out a hand. “Welcome. I’m Sarah Brown, one of the official greeters. Happy to meet you.”

I stared at the woman. She had dark skin and laughing eyes. Although probably in her mid-nineties, she seemed vigorous and sharp. How could this be? I didn’t want to be rude, so I just shook the proffered hand. She saw my confusion and said, “Ah. You must have been expecting something different. I understand. From what new residents tell me, the outside world thinks of this as hell. Clearly, that’s wrong.” A smile lit up her face as she looked around the sumptuous garden. “You can see for yourself.”

“How can that be? Isn’t this where people come to die?”

The woman laughed. “Well, yes and no. They do die here, of course. Nothing can stop that. But before we die, we live.” She spread her arms wide. “Everyone’s skills are needed, and people find that, when they’re needed, they rise to the occasion.”

I considered what I’d heard. It made sense, in a way, but that couldn’t be the whole answer. “Bullshit,” I said. “What’s the real reason?”

Sarah laughed so hard she bent double. “Walk with me,” she said when she had caught her breath. “I’ll show you to your apartment.

Number 42. That's a lucky number. Jackie Robinson's number, if you recall." Paul had followed baseball, so I recognized the name. But, I didn't respond. I was busy staring in wonder at the gardens. This place reminded me of a village in Italy Paul and I had visited long ago. It too had dazzled me with its soft beauty.

Sarah continued. "The state gives us adequate food for our population, so we don't really need to grow our own. We find that organic vegetables taste better, and it's important that food tastes good when you don't have a big appetite. The flowers lift the spirit."

She stopped, giving me an appraising look. "I don't know if you're a gardener or not…"

I shook my head.

"Okay. We don't have many rules here, but an important one is that everyone needs to make a contribution, based on their abilities and interests. I have an idea for you."

I waited to hear what she had to say.

"We need help writing a constitution. We call ourselves 'Empyrea,' meaning 'belonging to or deriving from heaven.' It's also a place in the DragonQuest games, but not many of us play that, so we just think of it as Heaven." She laughed. "A few residents are working on the constitution now, but they don't know much about that kind of thing. It's right up your alley. Interested?"

"Me? Write a constitution? Why?"

"Ah. People are living much longer than expected, and we need rules and laws. Perhaps you would like to be a judge, too? Even though we don't have much crime, there are disputes, and judges are always necessary. You can do whatever you choose, as long as you make a contribution. That's all that's required of our residents, at least for now. We've only been open for three years, so we're a work in progress."

"I…I hardly know what to say."

"Yes, everyone's a bit overwhelmed at first. I was in the initial group that settled this place, so for me it's home. I love it. Okay, here we are." She led me into a two story building and located number 42. Opening the door, I saw a small apartment not much different from the condo I'd just left, except for the sparse furnishings. A couch and loveseat, and a table and two dining chairs filled the space. No pictures on the walls and no mementos of the previous resident remained. It was far better than I'd expected. Sarah handed me a welcome packet. "Read this. It gives more information, and it tells when meals are served. Do you have any questions?"

This whole place so overwhelmed me that I could barely form a coherent thought, much less ask questions. I shook my head.

Sarah looked at her watch. "I have other people to greet, so I'll leave you to get settled. Dinner's at six. There's a map in your packet."

I finally found my voice. "Uh, how many people live here...in Empyrea?" I refused to call it Heaven.

"Right now, there are around 4,500 people."

"Are they all as…vigorous…as you?"

Sarah laughed again. "No, not all. Some are sick and others dying. But I would say that maybe sixty or seventy percent are like me."

"I don't mean to be rude, but…how can that be?"

Sarah nodded. "Eat dinner with me, and I'll tell you."

When Sarah left, I lay down to rest. The stress of leaving behind everything I knew had exhausted me. Still, this place was amazing, at least on the surface. I must be missing something. Maybe the horrendous aspects of the community were hidden away in dark cellars somewhere, so as not to scare the new arrivals. I would definitely investigate the next day.

At six, I joined a group of women and men heading to the cafeteria. They gave me a tour along the way. I saw a tiny library with two bookshelves filled with worn paperbacks, an exercise room with a few battered exercise machines, and a small general store that carried necessities like toothbrushes, socks and raincoats. It also sold those bright dresses that the women all seemed to wear. Hmm. A few suppliers must be allowed to bring in a small assortment of goods. Maybe I could use that knowledge in some way.

The pleasant hum of conversations coupled with the aroma of baking bread enticed me into the cafeteria. I selected a plate of cheese and crackers and looked around for Sarah. She sat at the front table, an empty chair beside her. When I joined her, she introduced me to the leaders of Empyrea. Everyone seemed pleased to meet the famous Congresswoman. I began to relax.

Sarah and I shared our life stories during dinner and lingered over cups of coffee. Finally, I said, "All right. I see old people who are full of energy and look healthy. Tell me why that is. It doesn't make sense."

Sarah nodded. "The woman who sat across from us? That's Dr. Chattahara. She joined us shortly after we opened. She had been a research scientist, and she was trying to develop an herbal remedy for arthritis. Fortunately for us, no drug company would sponsor it. So, she brought her research with her and set up a lab here. Well, she succeeded. It turns out that the herb works for many conditions, not just arthritis. It improves some forms of heart disease, reduces symptoms in Parkinson's, and completely cures Zika--both the old version and the new. She calls the remedy divyauSadha, meaning heavenly herbs. The rest of us can't pronounce that very well, so we just call it Strangelove. Not because of the old movie, but because it's so unlikely and so wonderful."

"Wait a minute," I said. "You said Zika. People all over the country—the world, actually—are terribly sick from Zika. My husband even died from it. Are you sure this herb cures the disease?"

"Yes, anyone who gets Zika is given a big dose of Strangelove. As far as I know, they all recover within three days with no complications. I had it myself, and I'm fine."

"But…that's amazing! Has she given it to anyone outside the wall?"

"No." Sarah sipped her coffee as she thought about it. "There's no communication with the outside world, as you know. Besides, she wouldn't do that, even if she could. Strangelove is our secret. There's only a small supply of it, and it's needed for our population."

"But if it really works as you say, it could change the world. If it can cure Zika, then we wouldn't need Empyrea. All of us could go home to our families."

"Maybe. But that world kicked us out, if you recall. I can't speak for everyone, but I like it here. People in here live longer than those on the outside without needing much in the way of medicine. When Strangelove fails, and it does eventually, we go to the clinic. Dr. Chattahara's team gives us something that makes us fall asleep, and that's it." She laughed. "The politicians thought they were punishing us for outliving our statistical probabilities, but instead they sentenced us to an early heaven. No, I don't see any reason to give Strangelove to the world."

"Look," I said. "I know I just got here, and I don't really understand this place. It just seems incredibly selfish to keep something this important from the rest of the world. Does everybody agree with you?"

Sarah shrugged. "I don't know. We've been having monthly votes, and anybody can put anything on the ballot. Majority wins. The Strangelove question hasn't come up." She sighed. "For thirty-five years I taught social studies in a high school in Baton Rouge. I wish more people would take an interest in the big issues. If they had, maybe this whole situation would have turned out differently."

"I still think..."

"We just had a vote last week," said Sarah, "so the next one won't be for another three weeks. Feel free to talk to our President about putting the Strangelove question on the next ballot. I don't think you'll win, but it would be interesting to see how it turns out." She paused. "Listen, you're new. When you've been here a while, you might understand that things aren't all black and white. I would ask you to get to know us before you decide how things should be. Give us a chance, all right?"

"Fair enough," I said. "I don't want to get off on the wrong foot in my new home. But this Strangelove seems to be a miracle drug. I think it should belong to the world. You don't know how bad it is out there. The hospitals are overcrowded, even though there's not much to be done, and people are dropping dead on sidewalks. Thousands of babies are born with tiny heads or neurological damage. They'll never be normal, no matter how much treatment they get. Oh, yes, I'll definitely put the issue on the next ballot." I stopped and took a breath as I tried to calm down. Eventually I managed to smile. "Meanwhile, I'll be happy to work with your committee on drafting a constitution. I'll even be a judge, if I'm elected. Or, appointed. However you do it."

"Great."

Back at my apartment, my mind swirled with possibilities. Sarah told me that the cafeteria workers added Strangelove to the desserts every night. Not every resident knew why they felt so good, and those who did know didn't talk much about it. I had the key lime pie, and so far I didn't feel any different. Sarah hadn't said how long the herb would take to start working. I was tired but no more than usual. Before I went to bed, though, I needed to call Chloe.

I took off the pin, pushed the center diamond, and heard a ringtone. Chloe answered immediately. "Grandma, you made it. How are you?"

I wanted to tell her all about Empyrea, including Strangelove. Especially Strangelove. But trying to explain this amazing place would have to wait until after I had done more research. "I made it, sweetie, and I'm fine. Listen, I've got to go. I might not call again right away. There are some things I need to find out first. I'll be in touch when I can. I love you. Bye." I pushed the diamond again. The pin went dark.

The next day, I walked through the entirety of Empyrea. Behind the chapel, I found a tall stack of cheap pine coffins. The newly dead were placed inside and loaded on the train for the trip back to civilization. I also visited the medical clinic, where a physician and a nurse treated a couple of patients for injuries they'd sustained from falls. In the medicine cabinet, I saw only aspirin and first aid supplies. The doctor shrugged when I asked about it. "We make do. In a way, it's almost like being a faith healer. We provide emotional support and what drugs we have. Either it's enough or it isn't. Basically, we are all dead when we arrive, according to the outside world. In a way, it's a relief to not have to try so hard to live as long as possible."

I wasn't sure what to think, so I thanked her and left. I visited the hospice, which housed a dozen people in various stages of dying.

It looked like other hospices I'd visited, except for the lack of medical equipment.

If Empyrea had a secret dark side, I didn't find it.

I joined the committee to draft Empyrea's constitution that afternoon. Three other women and one man were already working on it, but they hadn't gotten very far. One member had been diagnosed with cancer, which Strangelove didn't cure, so it was her last committee meeting. Before she left, she wanted to finish drafting the section about personal rights. "I feel strongly that all people should have the right to end their lives peacefully, when and how they wish, even here," she said. "Nobody should be able to take that right away."

The discussion went on for hours, with members bringing up items to include. "What about people with dementia? They can't take the potion themselves. Somebody else has to do it for them. How do you handle that?"

I loved this type of large, far-ranging debate. Paul and I had discussed every piece of legislation I'd sponsored, both in the state legislature and in the U.S. Congress, probing for weaknesses and unanticipated consequences. I'd sponsored a "right to die" bill numerous times, and it had failed each time. Here I was discussing it again with much more optimism. I savored the irony.

Three weeks flew by filled with activities. Sarah and I ate our meals together and discussed what needed to be accomplished in Empyrea. Our first effort was to initiate The Memory Project, where people recorded memories to be sent to their families upon death.

We brainstormed what else we needed, and I maintained a list of suggestions.

I felt better every day. Strangelove had definitely kicked in, but I didn't think that was the complete story. I felt more appreciated than I had in years. My skills were useful here. I felt so good that I procrastinated calling Chloe, telling myself I would call her soon. Just not yet.

The constitution committee hammered out several sections of the document to be put to a vote. One section for the next ballot included whether or not to give Strangelove to the world. Sarah and I held a debate about the issue one evening on the steps of the library. Only a few people attended, but I called on my oratorical skills to try to convince them to vote my way. I had witnessed firsthand the suffering that Zika caused, and I wanted to spare others that fate. My argument was simple and straightforward. "Isolating any group of people is wrong, and that's bad for society. Strangelove can save many lives. We can trade it for our freedom, and we'll be able to return to our families. Just because we're old doesn't mean we can't make a contribution there, just like we do here."

Sarah countered, "The young people put us out because we made them uncomfortable. We're doing fine here, in spite of them. Let the outside world do its own research and leave us in peace. Somebody else will come up with a cure for Zika."

At the end of the debate, those attending clapped politely and went on their way. I didn't think I had persuaded them. Maybe I needed a more personal approach. Over the next week, I talked to nearly every person in Empyrea, urging them to vote to give Strangelove to the world. Very few people agreed with me. They had made their peace with leaving that world and just wanted to enjoy the rest of their days.

Even so, I was convinced my arguments would persuade people when they thought more about it. Finally, the day of the vote arrived. That evening, the sympathetic expression on Sarah's face told me that I had lost. Damn. I hadn't been able to stop the IceFloe, either from the outside or from the inside. What was wrong with people? Or, was something wrong with me?

I grieved for a few hours, then realized I needed to call my granddaughter. Chloe would be out of her mind with worry. I shouldn't have put it off for so long. But, I had been sure I would have good news for her. Now I didn't know what I would say.

She answered immediately. "Grandma, are you okay? I've been staring at the phone, wondering why you haven't called."

"I'm fine, honey. I can't talk long. Somebody might be listening. Is everything all right with the family?"

"Not really. Do you get the news where you are?"

Even though Empyrea could receive radio and television news broadcasts, few people bothered with them. That life had ended. "We can. I haven't paid any attention lately. What's going on?"

"On a personal note, Seth and I got engaged a couple of weeks ago. Well, we did that because I found out I'm pregnant."

"Congratulations, sweetie. That's wonderful. My first great-grandchild. I'm sure you and Seth will be happy together." I paused. Something about her tone seemed off. "Uh, how are you feeling?"

"I'm okay right now. But I'm worried about Zika. It's hit our area really hard. I'm scared, Grandma. I wish you were here."

"Me too, sweetie."

"I spend most of my time indoors so I won't get bitten by mosquitoes. And I wear Deet all the time. But it's kind of hard to be a reporter and not go outside, you know?"

"Yes, I can imagine. Your baby is more important than your job, isn't it?" I wasn't sure how I would have answered that question in my twenties. My daughters would have said I always put the country's welfare before that of my own family. Chloe wasn't me, thank goodness.

"I plan on quitting as soon as things are settled with you. But, I can't leave until you're okay. My FBI contact is ready to break in there and rescue you whenever you give the word. What's the hold-up?"

At last, the moment I'd dreaded had arrived. I hadn't prepared a speech, so I took the coward's way out. "Oh, somebody's coming. I'm sorry, honey. I'll need to call you back. Wait to hear from me before you do anything, all right?"

I cut the connection and went for a walk, thinking about my options. On the one hand, I could tell Chloe about Strangelove and allow her team to break into Empyrea and rescue me. If I did that, my great-grandchild, as well as thousands of other children, could be born healthy. That in itself should be enough justification for giving the herb to the world. There would be no need for Empyrea. It was what I had come here to do, after all. But, as Sarah had said, things weren't always black and white. I wasn't as sure of myself as I had been when I first arrived.

On the other hand, if I told the world about Strangelove, Empyrea could lose control of it, and the government might choose to keep our residents from taking the herb. It had that power. If that happened, I would have been responsible for wrecking the place I had come to love. Without Strangelove, this sweet community might turn into the hell I'd expected to find when I arrived.

No one else in Empyrea had any idea of what was happening to loved ones. Just talking to Chloe had broken the rules, some of which I had written into the constitution. I'd insisted on setting up a small jail. If anyone found out what I had done, I might be its first occupant.

I walked and thought, walked and thought. Other ideas came to me. Maybe I could swear Chloe to secrecy and smuggle a bit of Strangelove out through the merchants who brought necessities into the community. Was that fair, saving my own family at the cost of losing so many other children? Of course not. Or, maybe I could negotiate the terms of sharing the Strangelove formula with the rest of the world. No, that wouldn't work because the vote had gone against me. Faith in the democratic process had sustained me throughout my life. I wasn't going to undermine that vote. Maybe, if

I didn't call Chloe back, my granddaughter's team would break into the compound and absolve me of responsibility for the decision?

Eventually, I sat on a bench beside a small hill and watched the stars erupt in the night sky. I thought about my life and what was left of it. Strangelove had helped me for a few weeks, but now I could feel my energy waning every day. I didn't have long. As much as I wanted to put off making this last big decision, I couldn't.

I acknowledged what I had to do as dawn broke. I had known all along, even as I argued with myself. No matter how hard I tried, I was still Lucy Underhill, who always did the right thing instead of what would be best for herself or her family.

Moving slowly, I detached the pin from my blouse, holding it in my hand until I felt its warmth. Then, I pulled back my arm and watched the pin sail through the air and over the wall.

I would be under the hill soon, but today I had much to accomplish. As the sun rose, I headed back home to start writing down my memories.

MATISSE IN WINTER

Kristine Mietzner

In the midst of winter, I found within me, an invincible summer. And that makes me happy. For it says that no matter how hard the world pushes against me, within me, there's something stronger – something better, pushing right back. -Albert Camus

Juneau, Alaska. 1966

Annette Halvorson leaned against the pillows, held her hand to the morning light, and admired her ruby ring with diamonds on each side of the stone. When Michael gave her the band last summer at Camp Lutherwood, he had promised that someday he would replace it with a wedding ring. She whispered the name, "Mrs. Michael Bennett," as she glanced outside her window at the homes and trees dotting Juneau's hillside. A north wind rustled through the aspens, sending golden leaves fluttering to the ground. The Fairweather mountains, framing the town, were dusted with snow. Fall was here.

Annette's mother walked into the room and sat beside her on the canopy bed. "You're still in bed. It's a school day. Are you sick?"

"I'm not feeling well, and I need to stay home."

"What's wrong?"

Annette took a deep breath and then blurted out the reason she didn't want to go to school, "I haven't had my period for three months." She wasn't sure what would happen now, but at least she'd told her mother the truth. Sabina often said there was nothing to be gained from delaying bad news.

Mom frowned and said nothing a few moments. "Have you been with someone?"

Annette hung her head and nodded.

Sabina gasped. "You're only sixteen."

Annette heard disappointment in her mother's voice. She prayed that Sabina wouldn't start shouting. Instead of raising her voice, her mom put her arm around Annette and said, "We won't go to a doctor in Juneau because someone we know might find out you had a pregnancy test. There are no secrets in small towns. We'll take the first flight to Seattle in the morning. Get busy and pack your suitcase. I'll call a doctor." Her mother left the room.

Annette inhaled deeply and slumped her shoulders as she exhaled. She'd finally told her mother about her missed periods. Mom seemed more sad than angry. Her reaction could've been far worse. Her friend, Cindy, had kicked her out of the house by her mother for getting pregnant. Cindy had to live with a family in Seattle who took her in out of pity.

If Annette were eighteen, she and Michael could get married. No one would point fingers and make judgments the way people did when a girl was unmarried, underage, and pregnant. Michael's father was a United States Senator who insisted his sons go into politics. What if Michael ran for office? If anyone knew that Michael had fathered a child with a teenager, it could only hurt his career.

Seattle, Washington

Annette woke to the rumble of the Alaska Airlines jet touching down at Sea-Tac. She drowsily inspected the airline cabin. Where was she? A glimpse of her mother's worried face reminded her why she and Sabina had come to Seattle. Her throat burned and her mouth felt dry.

She followed her mother to the taxi stand and remained silent on the ride to Dr. David Phillips's medical office downtown. Inside the waiting room, only a few minutes passed before Annette's name was called.

The middle-aged nurse handed Annette a plastic cup labelled *Annette Halvorson, 1-27-1950*. "Take this into the restroom and give us a urine sample. Leave it on the shelf, please."

Annette sat on the toilet and squeezed the cup between her legs. She caught some pee, placed the cup on the shelf, and exited to the hall. *I don't need a test to know I'm pregnant*, Annette thought glumly.

"All done?" the nurse asked as she glanced at her clipboard. Without waiting for a reply, the woman said, "Right this way," leading Annette and Sabina to an exam room. "I'm Nurse Simpson. I'll be assisting the doctor."

After taking Annette's pulse and measuring her blood pressure, the nurse said, "Here's a gown. Take off everything, including your bra and panties. The ties are in the front." Nurse Simpson patted the exam table. "Sit up here when you're ready. The doctor will be here soon."

"I'll wait outside while you change," said Sabina.

Annette donned the gown. Examining herself in the mirror, she ran her fingers through her short brown hair. Her mother returned to the room. While they waited, she and her mother thumbed through copies of *McCall's* and *Good Housekeeping* magazines.

"Good afternoon, ladies. I'm Dr. Phillips." With his blond hair, lanky frame, and kind face, he reminded Annette of her father. "Let's see what's going on. Scoot down a bit." The doctor did a physical exam, putting his hand between Annette's legs until his fingers slipped inside.

Annette called out, "Ouch!"

Dr. Phillips moved his hand several times asking. "Does this hurt?"

"Yes," Annette said.

"When was your last menstrual period?"

Annette closed her eyes. "The first week in July."

"When did you first have intercourse?"

Annette froze.

Sabina reached over and touched Annette's arm. "He needs to know, dear. No one else will know. I promise."

As she stared at the ceiling, Annette said, "Near the middle of July," and wished she could disappear.

The doctor removed his hand and stepped away. "Get dressed, go out to lunch, and come back to meet me this afternoon at one. We'll have the lab results and we'll know more."

That afternoon, Annette and her mother sat in the doctor's leather chairs and looked across a wide desk at Dr. Phillips.

"The pregnancy test was positive. From the physical exam and what you've told me, I believe you're nearly three months along."

Annette put one hand on her stomach and the other on her hip. *This should not be happening. They won't see me cry,* she promised herself.

He peered over his bifocals. "I understand you're not married."

Annette nodded and folded her arms. "I'm too young to be married. I made a mistake."

"Yes, I see," he said. Smiling at Sabina and then Annette, Dr. Phillips said, "In special cases like yours, when a pregnancy is medically dangerous, something can be done." He had a calm demeanor, a caring tone of voice, and he acted unhurried, as if he had no other patients.

Annette initially relaxed, sensing the doctor's compassion. Goosebumps rose on her arms. *Wait a minute,* she thought; *he's suggesting an abortion.* As the meaning of the doctor's words sank in,

Annette told herself to stay quiet and think before speaking. Her cheeks flushed, and her heart pounded.

"I thought that kind of thing was terribly dangerous." Annette closed her eyes and recalled the stories she'd heard–life-threatening infections, girls who could never again have children, severe pain, excessive bleeding.

As if reading her mind, the doctor said, "The general public only hears stories of the botched, so-called 'back-alley' operations. You, however, would be treated in a first-class hospital where I have privileges. Nothing bad will happen."

Annette disagreed. *Ending the pregnancy wasn't a good thing. Even if the procedure was safe, how could she live with herself?*

The doctor continued, "No one will ever know this happened. You'll have a second chance."

Annette shook her head, inspected Sabina's expressionless face, and spoke in a firm voice. "Dr. Phillips. Mom. I can't and won't do that. No."

Her mother placed a white-gloved hand on Annette's knee, then leaned forward to address Dr. Phillips. "Tell us more."

"With the help of a doctor, women and girls from families like yours can find a medical reason to justify having a procedure in a hospital. I will say it's medically necessary, and therefore the operation will be legal. This is exactly what I would recommend to my daughter. I would insist, in fact."

Annette crinkled her forehead. "You make ending a pregnancy sound like something that happens every day."

Sabina touched Annette's knee and said, "Don't be rude to the doctor. He's trying to help us."

Dr. Phillips replied, "Pregnancies are terminated every day for, let's say, medical reasons. There's nothing to be ashamed of."

With a calm voice and dry eyes, Annette, said, "No matter what, I want this baby to have a chance."

Annette's mother stood up and gripped the back of her chair. "What will people say? You will be called all kinds of names, even though you and I know that you were in love and didn't intend to get pregnant. It's unfortunate, but true: you'll be called a whore. You simply can't bring home a baby to Juneau. You'll lose your reputation, and mine could be ruined, too. Imagine what people would say if the French teacher's daughter was pregnant. I could lose my job." Her words ended in a gasp, almost a sob.

Standing up, Annette gathered the courage to say more. "I've heard there's a home for unwed mothers in Seattle."

Sabina waved away the idea. "That's not possible. Too many of our friends visit Seattle to go shopping. Someone might see you." Her mother sat down and sighed.

Annette leaned forward in her chair. "Dr. Phillips, where I can go?"

The doctor pulled open his desk drawer and picked up a pen and a small black notebook. "Let me give you some phone numbers. There are homes for unwed mothers in Portland, San Francisco, and other cities. A number are called Crittendon homes, and the Catholic Church operates others. Some families, those who can afford to do so, send their daughters to Europe." He gazed steadily at Annette's mother.

Sabina smiled widely and picked up her purse. "Thank you, Dr. Phillips. You've given me an idea." Her tone had changed from troubled to cheerful.

Copying her mother, Annette lifted her handbag from the floor. The doctor and Annette turned to Sabina and waited for her explanation.

"The nuns in Vence, France -- the town where I grew up -- run a high school. Their convent is next door. I can ask them if Annette can live there."

"Very well. You have the beginnings of a plan. You can work out the details." He closed Annette's file and looked up. "If things don't work out with the convent, call my office and we'll help place Annette in a home for unwed mothers somewhere in the United States."

"Thank you so much," Annette's mother said.

"You're welcome, Mrs. Halvorson." He turned toward Annette. "Go home and take good care of yourself. You won't show for a while, so you have time to make arrangements."

Tears rolled down Annette's face on the flight home to Juneau.

Her mother whispered, "Now, now. Don't cry. Your eyes will be puffy. I want you to hold your head high and act as if everything is normal. Do you understand? You'll tell your friends how much you're looking forward to a year as a Rotary Club exchange student."

After a long pause, she said, "About the baby's father. It's time for you to tell me his name."

Annette lifted her chin slightly. "We're in love. I'm not telling anyone his last name. No need to ruin two reputations."

The stewardess poured tea into china cups and handed the drinks to Sabina and Annette. As the flight attendant moved to the next row

Annette's mother sipped her tea. "I can understand that you want to try and protect the father because you're a kind person. I admire that about you." Taking Annette's hands in hers, she said, "For the baby's sake, it would be better if the birth father's name was on the paperwork. When the baby is born, you'll be far away. No one in Juneau will need to know his name. No one will know you had a baby."

Annette turned away and stared out the window. *She would know, and she would never forget.* She pressed her face against her mother's shoulder, unable to stop crying.

Sabina said, "We'll get through this."

"Mom, I know you mean well, but you have no idea how bad I feel."

Sabina put an arm around Annette and squeezed her close. "I do know, because something similar happened to me." She dabbed a tissue on Annette's tears.

Annette pulled the Kleenex from Sabina's hand and looked at her mother. "Did you give up a baby for adoption?"

"Yes." Sabina peered past her, through the window.

"I thought you met Dad in France and got married right away."

"We did. There was someone else, before I met your father. During the war I fell in love with a man who was a few years older than me. Our parents didn't approve, because my family was Catholic and he was a Jew."

"What are you saying? What happened?"

Sabina took a deep breath and put her hand over Annette's. "If it works out for you to go to my hometown, you'll see a monument in the center of town. Inscribed on the stone are the names of each one of the Jews that was rounded up and executed by the Nazis. One of those Jews was my boyfriend, and the father of my first child." Sabina sighed. "Now you know my truth."

Annette saw the tears in her mother's eyes and squeezed her hand. "Does Daddy know?"

Sabina drew away, nodded, and wiped away her own tears. She tilted her head and patted Annette's hand. "Yes. For a long time, we sent money to the family who raised her. Not a day goes by that I don't think about her."

"Do you still send money?"

"We stopped when she joined a convent."

"What is her name?"

"Rachael was her given name, but she has a new name as a nun." Sabina folded her hands, and closed her eyes.

"Please, tell me more."

"When the time is right."

Juneau, Alaska

Two nights later, Annette heard a vehicle crunching the gravel in the driveway. She pulled back her bedroom curtains and saw her dad's pick-up parked there. Annette took pride in in her father's career as a pilot for Alaska Airlines. He stepped out of his white truck, looking as handsome as he always did in his uniform. She released the curtains and resumed pacing the floor. Annette dreaded the conversation they were about to have.

The positive pregnancy test, the suggested abortion, and the flight had been exhausting, but facing Dad would be worse. Annette's chest tightened.

The screen door slammed shut. Annette settled into the captain's chair at the desk where she did her homework, a task that now seemed forever unimportant. She imagined her mother conveying the bad news. Minutes passed. Her father's heavy footsteps sounded in the hall, and then there were taps on the door.

"Buddy? Are you taking visitors?"

That was good. If he were angry, he would have used her full name.

Annette's father sat on the edge of the bed, reached out, and held her hands in his. "My little girl is all grown up." He released her hands, flexed his fingers, and made fists.

Annette's heart pounded hard as she waited.

After a few moments, he said, "Your mother called the Dominican convent in Vence. She's made arrangements for you to stay there until the baby arrives."

Annette stood and faced her father. "I could raise the baby here." Even though her mother said it was impossible, maybe Dad would go along with the idea.

Paul spoke in a sad and tired tone. "The nuns will find the baby a good home."

"No!" Annette grabbed her father's shoulders. "I want to keep the baby. No one can make me give up the baby!" Annette pushed her father.

He moved backward slightly but quickly regained his straight posture. She started swinging her fists against the bed. Her father caught Annette's thrashing arms and held her tightly, until, at last, she stopped. They sat beside each other on the bed. Annette pressed her head against her father's chest and stared at the floor.

"Annette, you're too young to be a mother. In a perfect world, I'd like for you to keep the baby, too. We need to do the right thing. The child will have the best chance with parents that are ready to have a family."

Devastated, Annette wrapped her arms around her waist and stared at her father with disbelief. His eyes were watering. She had never seen him cry.

Her father's hands rested on his knees. He took a deep breath, exhaled, and said, "The nuns asked for a large donation. They want you to work as a kitchen helper. Can you do that?"

"Yes, of course."

"When I find out the name of the boy who did this, I'm going to have a talk with him and his parents. He can't get away with this. He should take some responsibility. If nothing else, he and his parents can share in this so-called donation. What's more, I'm going to give them all a piece of my mind."

Annette gasped. "Dad! Don't! Please don't cause a scene."

"I'll find out who got you pregnant, if it's the last thing I ever do."

Annette's heart sank. Most of the time, Dad kept his promises.

"Things are bad enough. I don't want to destroy his life. Don't. Don't bring him into this."

"Too late for that. Annette, you're not even old enough to consent to sex."

Annette pulled on the sleeve of her father's jacket and leaned into him, resting her head on his shoulder. "Talking to his parents won't change anything. Can't you leave things alone? I love him. He's going to be a lawyer, and I want him to finish school. If he knows I'm pregnant, he might drop out of law school, get any old job, and then he'd resent me and the baby for the rest of his life."

"I don't care what he does, as long as he stays away from you. I agree with your mother that his name should be on the birth certificate. A child deserves that much. Listen, Buddy, you'll have to be strong to get through this. I know you can do it." He put his arm around her and squeezed her toward him. "Your mother will take you to Vence and return to pick you up after the baby is born. That's the plan." He stood up and rested his eyes on her again, then strode out of the room.

If only she could keep the baby! But her parents were right. She would be considered used goods and never get a husband if she raised a baby alone, and she had no job skills. She didn't have enough money to raise a child.

Vence, France. 1967

Annette would tell no one about the baby until the time was right, not even Michael, the baby's father. As she rested on a wooden chair, with her hands clasped around her large belly, violet shapes danced on the Matisse Chapel's white walls, refractions from the stained-glass windows.

The shimmering rectangles reminded her that she was missing the Valentine's Day dance back home in Juneau. A dangling mirror ball would flicker light around the ballroom, just like those windows were doing now. Annette circled her hand over her stomach and closed her eyes.

Michael would have flown in from Seattle to be her date. The yearning she had tried to push away rushed to the surface. Why hadn't he answered her letters?

Moments later, soft footsteps approached and starched fabric rustled, sounds that could only belong to Sister Marie, the one English-speaking nun, and Annette's only friend at the convent.

Annette watched as the woman sat down on the chair beside Annette. "You're such a lovely girl," said the nun. "Has anyone ever told you that you look like Audrey Hepburn?"

"My mother, for one. I miss her." Annette twisted the ring on her right hand. "When I first got here people called out, 'Audrey!' when I walked by. But now I'm too big for that kind of thing. I look like a whale."

"How are you feeling? Your morning sickness should be over by now."

Annette frowned and looked up sharply. "How would you know? You've never been pregnant." The words sounded harsher than she had intended.

Sister Marie paused for a moment and leaned forward, bowing slightly. "Many women have walked your path and found their way."

The nun's gentle tone and kind eyes touched Annette. "I'm sorry. Maybe you were like me at some point in your past. I don't really know your story."

"You have a good imagination, but, no, Annette, I came to the convent as a teenager. My mother was like you, though. She was young and unmarried when I was born."

Annette's temples throbbed. She pressed the fingertips of both hands to the sides of her head. "I didn't mean to be rude. It's just that I didn't want this to happen. My life was supposed to be different."

She passed her hand across her belly again. "I got into this mess all by myself. Well, not quite." Thinking of Michael, she lowered her head, and after a few moments, lifted her chin and looked at the nun. Tears covered Annette's face. "I don't want to give up my baby, but keeping it would bring shame to my family. My mother might lose her job."

"One day, the child will want to know about her mother. This person will grow up and find you, eventually."

Sister Marie's cheerful, confident suggestion made Annette turn and look at her more closely.

The nun nodded toward the side of the chapel and gestured with one hand at the larger-than-life, line drawing on the white-tiled wall, depicting Mary holding a toddler-sized Jesus. "See the right side? Matisse used one line for both Mary and Jesus."

As Annette gazed at the drawing, the baby kicked hard. She jumped, and her eyes widened. "It moved!" Glancing from the image of the mother and child to her own protruding belly, she considered the idea. Even if they were physically separated, just like the painting, they would share one line.

Now the nun pointed to a stained-glass window. "The green shapes in the windows depict cactus leaves and symbolize the Tree of Life. The translucent blue panes are the sky. The yellow panes are opaque, the light doesn't shine through them, but the light does shine through the blue and green."

"The light is beautiful." Annette squeezed the nun's hand. "I wish I could stay longer, but I have to go help Jacques prepare dinner." She stepped back, but the nun didn't release her grip

"Wait a moment. There something more I need to tell you." The nun leaned forward with a look of intensity on her face that Annette hadn't seen before. She looked Annette in the eyes. "Sometimes, God doesn't speak to us directly, but talks to us through others."

"Yes, of course, Sister. But what are you getting at?"

The nun glanced around the chapel as if to make sure they were alone. She then lowered her head and folded her hands as if she intended to pray “Listen carefully to whatever Jacques tells you in the kitchen. He may be able to help you in some way.”

“I will. Thank you.” Annette rose with some difficulty because of her swollen belly and legs. As she walked slowly toward the chapel door, she touched the white tile wall to keep her balance. Just before stepping into the afternoon sun, Annette glanced back at the winter light dancing on the white walls. The young nun sat with bowed head, praying silently.

Annette followed the stone path to the convent kitchen. She sighed heavily. If only she and Michael had waited. Last summer, all she wanted was to have him in kissing distance.

Made in the USA
San Bernardino, CA
20 September 2017